Never Mind The Beasts

Never Mind The Beasts

Marcus Slease

Dostoyevsky Wannabe Originals
An Imprint of Dostoyevsky Wannabe

First Published in 2020
by Dostoyevsky Wannabe Originals
© Marcus Slease

Dostoyevsky Wannabe Originals is an imprint of
Dostoyevsky Wannabe publishing.

www.dostoyevskywannabe.com

Cover design by General Mathematics

ISBN-978-1-8380156-0-2

. . Yet this novel is not autobiography wearing a thin disguise of fiction, but rather, something more complex- fiction created out of real life, based on the experiences and beliefs of its author, and presented in the guise of autobiography . . this material has been altered, recombined, shaped to create a coherent and meaningful artifact, a crucial alchemy- art's transformation of life . . a principal subject and theme of this book.
— **Lydia Davis (introduction to Proust's Swann's Way)**

Two truths approach each other. One comes from the inside, the / other from the outside, / and where they meet we have a chance to catch sight of / ourselves.
— **Tomas Tranströmer**

There are too many birds / in your piano
— **Vincent Huidobro**

Contents

Never Mind The Beasts

The Troubles, bombs & rumours of bombs, the town blown up and then patched together again, the people also, if they're lucky. His mother, aged 17, hears a voice, the pain is for the purification, being born out of wedlock with the tug of metal forceps, the baby, someday, has a mission.

He walks to the back of the bus and folds his arms. Everyone has their kilted trolleys, a little pad, they lick the pencil and do the jottings, a day at the racetracks. Clomp clomp clomp of the black boots. He slips down and nuzzles into the lion's mane of the lady next to him. They find him anyway, take him into the police station, he folds his arms. What's your name wee pet, says the policewoman. He slides down in his seat, folds his arms, wrinkles his nose. I don't talk to police, he says. He folds his arms forever and ever. They bring him some marshmallow hedgehogs, a wagon wheel, a double decker. He tells them his name, but not his true name.

Back at home, a knock on the door. It's the police, says the dad. The dad comes into the toilet, keep your head down, he says. He keeps his head down, watches them cello-tape the bullets under the sofa. Later, in the evening, the dad is foaming at the mouth and strangling his mother. His uncle shows up with the church people, tries to expel the demons. The dad disappears for 26 years.

It is 1981, a bright summer day, the bakery windows steamy with the rising heat of sweet buns, the church & jewelers, at the bottom of the street, with their promises. The mothers and their prams, the fathers in the chicken factory, the bridge, in British colours, the trolls that sit under it. On the banks of the river with Buckfast, the story of bodies, so many, floating back in history, so long. & then the wail, it slices the ears, the rumble from somewhere near the centre, the mothers with their prams, running away or toward, it is hard to know the difference, the sweaty panic. Suddenly something hard & bloody, blue jeans, two legs, no body, a van, the man at the wheel screaming silently. Frozen, with chocolate buttons, sprinkles, so colourful, his favourite from Woolies.

He tries drawing a diamond and can't draw a diamond. He fails the test, shame, shame, shame. The psychologist pulls out a big piece of white paper, can you write an 8, he asks. He draws two circles joined together, begins to write backwards, no good with his hands. The lids, he can't peel them, he pokes them.

He plays in the mud with his Tonkas. He's a dirtyweeskitter. He's bin stuck in the muck all wick, says his aunt.

His Granda brings the budgies. The birds are slightly musty. His uncle jumps out of the wardrobe with an alien. Out come the creamies into the Cocoa Krispies, better when it's warm, on the stove from Granny, hot cocoa and soggy rice bits, the perfect start.

At the height of The Troubles, living in the homeless shelter, in South London, near Elephant and Castle, a man invites his new father for beer. He sips a few sips. Higher or lower, higher or lower, says the white toothed man on the telly. He has a belly at sea, swishing and swooshing, released into a blue bucket, people keep saying THE DOLE. *

Boys and girls play ring games in many parts of the world. During pre-teen years ring games are a precursor to adult courtship, players form a ring by holding hands, then one girl or boy goes into the middle of the ring and starts skipping or walking around to the song. The girl or boy is asked "show me your motion" and the child in the centre does their favourite dance. If asked "show me your partner," they pick a friend to join them in the circle. He has the wrong accent. He does not have "good motions." He does not have "show me your partner." After "his motions" the circle becomes a line, he walks down the line & all the girls on the estate pull his blond mop of hair.

At the street of crocodiles his skin is peeling away from his trousers. The ants swarm his shins. A man in yellow teeth leans over him. Please tick here. He ticks. Please tick here, he ticks. Please tick here, he ticks, please tick here. He ticks and ticks and ticks. They hang his knee and tap it with a glass hammer. They hang his biceps and stretch it with a rubber band. Oil him up and slap it. Yellow jello. OK, she says, please retire to the theatre. He is taken to a room with many mothers weeping. They press their faces against the glass doors. Are you sure you weren't on a bike, they ask. Not on a bike, he says. The straw is sticking out of his head. They bang his coconut. Are you sure you weren't on a bike, they ask. Not on a bike, he says. They bang his coconut. His untidy eyes, which way to point them. His untidy hands in his pockets. The wet puddles slicked with rainbows. The breezy wind that bends the branches.

His thick eyebrows catch a chill. Take my hand, she says. His bedroom is covered in glow in the dark stars. They scatter the toys on the floor, a boiling cauldron of hot lava, the toys are steppingstones, a crunch here and there, but nothing broken, keep hopping, try to make it to the sea. The sea is the bedspread, they swim together, a private island. A small boat approaches, the oars slap the water, it is the boat of the dead, but not really. It is a glass slipper. You have to float across, she says. He climbs inside and floats and floats. The sun sinks and the stars slink across the sky. The water is choppy. The glass slipper sinks and floats. He is feeling shivers rather than chivalry. Hold your breath, she says, you have to make your lungs bigger. He pumps his lungs, up and down, up and down, up and down. You can do it, she says. There is sand gritting his elbows and knees. He clambers around the island. Mouth salty, socks salty, ears and eyes salty. In the corner a thicket. Please, she says. He picks the blackberries, a whole bucket, pricked and scabbed over, when you tackle a blackberry it is very thorny. The ancient Blackberries, ramblers not climbers. The juice squirts the teeth. It is very bloody. They carry the basket of blackberries, his hand on the left handle, her hand on the right, and cross the street. They are on the island of a roundabout, waiting to cross, but the cars keep circling like sharks. They are on the island, waiting to cross. Swishhhhh. Swishhhhhhhh. Swishhhhh. It is time to play the game without getting hit by the cars.

You are a thief, trapped in a vault, with Stiffy, Scaredy, Smarty, & Silly. Eat the gold quickly before the police catch you. Blind alleys and loops. Banquet halls and kings. Gods and hideous monsters. Dust yourself with the stars of the night sky. One room leads to another.

His mother unlatches the blue door. The Thames rolls its tongue against the crumbling grey bricks, holds its silt, preserves the artefacts. To become silted is to: become blocked, become choked, become clogged, fill up (with silt), become filled, become damned. He visits the local, tells them stories. Vinegar drips from the chips and sogs the newspaper. He has come from very far away, another planet, his face full of freckle clusters. He slips off the bar stool, makes the rounds, from one wooden table to another, everyone loves his wiggle. Unlatching the gate, or climbing over, there are many bends in the river.

He was born under the sign of Aries with restless birth winds. She rubs his hair. Bricks in the oven, pulled out, put together with a tasty filling. Around & around with little boxes, if you smoke please try Carlton. She tries Carlton. He gets a Mars bar. They watch the balloons, not the little ones, the big ones. You stand in a basket, the hot flame shoots you into the sky. The rain patters into mud muddles. The port o potties are tilted. She takes his hand, the blue colouring of the lolly drips down his chin. Someone is standing on it, next to the meat truck, a pound note. Under one foot and then another, he waits for it, the wind kicks it away. A hairy stranger blows smoke through the nose, a thick fingered stranger counts back the coins. Try not to draw too much attention, you don't want someone else to spot it. He makes himself smaller and smaller, in and out of the crowds, he tries to catch it, the wind kicks it away.

They become a five-person family, a small green hill behind them, the Milton Keynes Bowl in the distance. Milton Keynes, the first American mall with a rocket ship, spewing blue and yellow smoke, playing Neil Diamond. We are coming to America today today. He looks at the rocket ship and his mum looks at him, they have won the lottery, they are going to America, but not on a rocket ship, and not today. At the swing set, singing and swinging, wondering if he is going to flip over. There is something in the air, a foggy sound from another planet. It is Major Tom. He is stepping through the door, floating in a peculiar way. The stars look different today.

The next door neighbour wins the race, the fastest sprinter. His favourite the ®egg and spoon race, followed closely, in second place, by the sack race. The mum does the three-legged race. In the evening the spaceship arrives full of buttercups. Every person is named Buttercup. Beam me up, Buttercup. Who's afraid of the goblins.

At the roundabouts the howls of foreign critters. The mangy cries and whispers. Bow down ten times or more with the furry temple in the distance. When your right eye twitches God is watching you. You've come so far and we can take you further. A man with wild hair smashes watermelons on the television. What do we need for existence? Two hydrogens, one oxygen. Fire from a star at just the right distance.

He looks at the tub, it is full of memories. What was your tub routine? The tiniest babies aren't ready. You have to wait until their stump has fallen off. You can sponge bath and after the loss you can start a new routine. Clear glass and sharp objects away from the sink, also bottles & razors from the sides of the tub. When you use soap the infant gets slippery, stroke the baby with washcloth, not rub or scrub, place in water gently. Lower feet first, speak in slow, low tones, cup hand over forehead, keep suds out of eyes. At lunchtime, egg and onion sandwiches, the wrong kind, a stink bomb, the giggles. She has thick glasses, he pulls out her chair. At home, the butter craters the toast and beans sog it, a great banger, dip it in brown sauce. He asks the mother to take a bath together, no, she says, you can't do that, you're too old. They are not babies, and not adults, and not teenagers, they can't take a bath together. They look at the tub, sharing and caring, sailing or rubber ducking, submerging, scrubbing and rubbing, the floaties.

Genghis knew a good pet when he saw one. The Mongolian gerbil is a claw warrior or a sleeping emperor. I don't want to, he says, holding the gerbil. But you have to. The gerbil runs into the fields and is eaten quickly. There is a hidden ear among the grass blades. You have to listen carefully.

He puts everything together slowly. In the lunchroom, mashed potatoes. Everything goes into it. The head teacher, curly haired and stubby, pokes him in the chest. You are not a cement mixer, he says.

Football, two jumpers for goalposts, the ground prickly with jack frost. He plays substitute, retires to a corner to kick his own ball, into the bushes, pop. When they sit down for a break they see it, the popped ball. Did he do it, they ask, pointing at an older boy riding past on a bicycle. His blood rushing, he says yes.

They crowd around the boy on the bicycle.
You popped his ball you wanker, they chant.
Here, they say, holding him, punch him, punch him.
It wasn't me, he says.
They crowd around the boy on the bicycle.
Punch him punch him, they chant.
The crowd is getting larger, he is the centre of attention.
They crowd around the boy on the bicycle.
It wasn't me, he says.
Punch him punch him, they chant.
It wasn't me, he says.
You wanker, they say.
Punch him, they say.
Admit it, says one.
You wanker, says another.
Punch him punch him, they say.
He doesn't want to punch him.
They crowd around the boy on the bicycle.
Punch him you wanker, they chant they chant.

At Bletchley, the swimming pool, a water slide, one pound if you go down it, says the new father.

But he can't do it.

One pound for diving, from the edge, with your knees spread apart for your hands to form a prayer, says the new father.

But he can't do it.

No matter, ping pong and hot chocolate, from the machine, his first taste.

Hard work brings blessings. The smell of cleaning agents. All is in order. Cleanliness is next to godliness. How to turn a boy into a man. You have to learn the stoic. At age 22 his new father, with the extra package. It comes with the territory, a small boy from another marriage, a little helper, doing the dishes, babysitting and cleaning. The new father rides his bicycle to the train station, for a job in London, driving the trains in the underground, the pink line, or purple, depending on how you are looking. The new father, at first patient, then less, sit up straight, eat everything on your plate. The gravy goes lumpy, the mash potatoes cold, the liver and onions rubbery, but worst of all the Brussels sprouts, a gas bomb, he has to finish it.

There is someone in the bushes, hugging a bottle, their feet sticking out. They kick him in the ribs, roll him over, kick him some more, the pleading, no drunks allowed, they chant. He pleads, but they keep kicking. He retires to the fields, and a little further, the hole. He peers into it. His secret stash, a red journal, the ink soggy. Scrubbing under the skin, it is hard to scrape it. He can never feel clean. Beneath the ink, more ink, smudged forever.

He is taken to the kitchen where she bakes and smokes, bakes and smokes.

The hot oven.

The clank of her wine bottles, Worzel Gummidge on the telly.

The clank of the wine bottles.

Piddling his trousers.

Hiding behind the couch with the play dough, salting and eating it.

Fiddling with it.

Fiddling with it.

Over and over.

The smell of play dough on his fingers.

The same dream.

Fiddling with it.

Over and over.

The smell of play dough on his fingers.

Until later, then he changes it, throws her down the stairs, breaks her neck.

Don't come back, this is my dream.

At the playground, there is Banana Kick Jamie, a prodigy maybe, very popular, and also tall, and also Jonathan, a recent convert to another religion, no birthdays or Christmas, just as strict as the Mormons. A burning fag on the footpath, Jamie picks it up, sucks it, on a dare, it's like candy for adults, his mum said. He pretend smokes with dry twigs. One day someone throws a large rock through an old woman's window. He hears the smash and everyone scatters. The old lady comes close, screeches in his face, tell your mates I'll call the police. He piddles his trousers, a warm leg and then a yellow puddle. He has to prove something.

After the conversion, they watch E.T. with the branch. The branch is a small gathering. If it is a larger gathering it is called a ward. They don't have a ward. They have a branch. It is a bootleg copy and the sound isn't synced. In the movie they are eating something called Pizza Hut. It is not liver and onions and potatoes. It is not pork chops and potatoes. It is not the fatted lamb with mint sauce and potatoes. It is not a shepherd's pie with mashed potatoes. It is not eels with potatoes. It is not bubble and squeak with potatoes and leftover vegetables. It is not at 7-Eleven. What is it?

His mum hides the WOW comics for him and he comes to collect them. During her smoke break, the new father comes with a used Chopper, his first bike. Manufactured and marketed in the 1970s, the design was influenced by dragsters, chopped motorcycles, beach buggies, and even chariots. The new father runs behind him holding onto the seat and then, close to the crab apples, with their prickly skins, he lets go. When he turns around his new father is waving. He pedals a bit further, crashes into a light pole. Viola. Independence. Spinning out and spinning in, the mud puddle splashes and bunny hops. It doesn't matter. At the oak, he curves around the tree, his knees scrapping the footpath. In the fields, he whips the wheat stalks with his hands.

Everyone lives in government housing, with the dole. The new father gets a new job in the new church, it is called a calling. His calling is to convert more converts. Pre-knotted brown ties and almost starched shirts, the rush forward, for something better, here now, and also, more importantly, later, in the heavens. You start sinning at 8, sinning is infinity. The spirit is supposed to stay white, go inside & give it a scrub. The water is cold, his new father holds up his hand in a square, it looks like a slap, his foot keeps coming out of the water. He was always dirty. 8 is the beginning of wisdom.

In Coffee Hall you might get away with a different coloured door, but mostly not, in an estate for the poor you shouldn't feel too special, just lucky, you climbed to the top of the government waiting list. Here is the toothbrush lesson. Close your eyes. Count to 60. Count to 60. Count to 60. That's how long to brush your teeth, says Miss Foster. You're a great reader, says Miss Foster. He didn't know it. He is good at something. His favourite teacher. At Christmas, the musical *Jesus Christ Superstar*. The mother writes the letter and Miss Foster reads it. She touches his shoulder. His face is on fire. It is against his religion. The wrong Jesus. He is not a rock star.

In Coffee Hall, with Terry and Wayne, riding bicycles, making the ramps with cardboard and bricks, jumping through fire hoops, playing American football with bomber jackets, stuffed at the shoulders with socks, tackling each other on the concrete, and later, back to rugby, with the coach, his nose crooked, broken eight times, that's what you get for playing rugby. After school, Terry, the older one, gets the whiskey from his mum, and they try the whiskey, in the trees beside their fort. He swishes and spits, it is against his religion but he doesn't tell them, he says it is better when you swish it, it seeps into your cheek, goes deeper. They all swish and spit, swish and spit, swish and spit, don't swallow.

White, stubby, and easily carried. Sturdy. The slot on top narrow. Every few days, the clank, at first hollow, and then more heavy, he is good at saving the pennies, and now and again his favourite, although he hates to let it go, the new 20p coin, an equilateral curve heptagon, something special. On Guy Fawkes, more plops. Also at Christmas, and for a while, some extra for the tooth under the pillow. Now it is full, you can't open it, you have to smash it, with a hammer.

For over a year, which has felt like 20, he has been waiting to smash it. How can he smash it? He needs a hammer, but he doesn't know where, or even if they have one, but they must have it. There are pictures of the prophet on the wall, and also family portraits, hanging by a nail, probably. There has to be a hammer. He walks into his mother's wardrobe, past the jeans and floral dresses, no hammer, but there has to be a hammer. In the cupboards, rice krispies and corn flakes, Farley's Rusks and Bovril, salt and pepper, no hammer. At night, and also first thing in the morning, he imagines it, the coins spilling out of it, the sound and feel of them, shiny, something he has waited for, his very own treasure.

Over the fence and down the damp alleys. The memories peeled and whittled, boiled and buttered, it is never the same later. The millennium is so far away, the future and past are illusions, very good. The decades are not measured evenly. The shaggy carpet, everything more hairy in the early 80s. Mrs Tittle Mrs Tittle, where is your golden apple. The shiny wrappers piled on the couch with various shapes and sizes. Try not to eat all the chocolate. The selection box with Curly Wurly and the Beano annual. Pull the lever at the bottom and they tumble into chaos, clink and clack, clink and clack, clink and clack. His mother has arrived with the food, the rustle of plastic bags, baked beans on the counter, spuds under the water, the knife from the drawer to peel them, around and around, the strips of gritty skin. He sees it, or the shape of it, round and white with crab like pincers at the front. A Millennium Falcon, probably. He does not want to see it, doesn't want to spoil it, but also wants to touch it, closes his eyes and feels it, imagines the tiny figures inside it, the deep space adventures they will have together.

Howling Dogs and Crinkled Whispers

The trailer park is full of lawn chairs. The slats are broken. Where do they come from? His other name is Silcock, a thrush, Anglo Saxon. But some say Huguenot. What is a Huguenot? His identity is a knot. It buckets down. No one can understand them. Where's the bap. How's your ma. How's your wee uns. A dander down to find the sweeties. They are called Hershey's. She takes a bite & then he takes a bite. The mum says, wax. He looks at the mum & says, wax. One more time, in unison, wax. But it is OK, it is still something like chocolate. A dander past the trailers, howling dogs & crinkled whispers. A half-eaten dumpster.

In Vallejo, in the trailer park, a blue light flashes, & they run to rip through the clothes. The mum says sorry sorry if she bumps into someone. It is not the American way, no sorries, elbows needed. It is the day of the blue light special & he acquires his first American burger. He had something like an American burger back in Milton Keynes. It tasted like cardboard. Thin grey and dry. Now hamburger, in America, from the source. & behold it is big, seedy and puffy, & there are many sauces. It doth cover most of his face, and it makes him exceedingly glad! In America, everything gets bigger and bigger, & they get smaller and smaller. In America, everything gets bigger & bigger and they can't get their mouth around it.

The small radio says Texas Rangers. Strawberry cornmeal gruel for breakfast. At school free lunch. Gird up your loins. The nerf football is half eaten. The new grandfather, a double war veteran, accepts him, but the grandmother, rejects, or is preoccupied, an unhappy marriage. The trailer is small but they all fit there, watching the television, planning for the future. They sit on the couch full of holes. For four months, every night in the trailer, it is the meat helper, flakey noodles and packet sauce and ground cow. They watch the adverts on the telly with the helping hand, a white glove with a red nose and a smiley face, like a talking snowman, but it isn't a snowman, it is a talking hand, for the meat helper.

He learned the stoic from the English, now he is learning from the Americans, one of these is gumption, it has the word gum in it. It is spirited initiative, outward facing, resourcefulness, supreme confidence, but you need the right conditions, the right conditions are maybe essential. Don't sugar-coat your life. Look at pictures of Jesus, imagine bleeding from every pore, don't sugarcoat it, baptise it. The gum balls are big like everything in America, red white & blue, monster gum balls. The gum balls in the gum ball machine are all about American presidents. You put in a nickel and out pops a card with the face of a president. Underneath the picture of the president there are facts: where they were born, what they were known for, and most importantly, their number. He tries to remember the chronology of the American presidents, in order to become an American citizen. He cannot blow a bubble, his mouth is not full of bodacious bubblicious or righteous Bazooka bubbles, it is full of the gum balls of American presidents. He tries to read the instructions, not from the gumball machine, somewhere else, like on a bubblicious packet. Many bubble blowing experts suggest removing the sugar without chewing the gum for too long. To do this, chew the gum for five minutes, then take it out of your mouth and hold it under warm, running water, while you are rolling it into a ball. Don't sugarcoat it, baptise it. Remember that large bubbles are so fragile that even the slightest breeze will make it pop. Just be careful when it pops, as all bubbles must. You need a cozy place to blow your bubbles. Blow bubbles inside, at perfect room temperature, with your family. This is called utopia. Don't sugarcoat it, baptise it. There is no end to blowing bubbles, or maybe there is. There is definitely an end of one bubble and the beginning of another. Chase the bubbles, &, in America, there is supposed to be plenty of bubbles, you just have to have gumption and blow your own bubble. Don't sugarcoat it, baptise it.

He looks in the mirror. I am almost a banana, he thinks. Everyone plays kickball or tetherball or four square or nerf football. He is not a team person. He is supposed to be a team person. He prefers to stand by the monkey bars. General rule of thumb: the less people the better. At night he dreams dreams of giants & hears the sound of a large foot stomping. It shakes the puffy clouds above him & he keeps climbing and climbing. At the monkey bars his red- haired friend, short and centred, hangs upside down, flips, & always finds her feet. His feet are far away. His toes are too big for his body. He learns how to type with Mavis, put your fingers here, your other fingers there, spread 'em, hands and feet, spread 'em, hands and feet, spread 'em. While you were sleeping we remade and improved you, says something far off, something beyond the shaking clouds.

They have moved to Vegas, away from the trailers. The father lays insulation. Let's drive the strip, says the mum. The strip, what is it? Glowing lights, earthly heavens, another kind of magic. Look, says the mother, tigers. Their owners, Siegfried and Roy, are very elegant. The tigers are white and fluffy with big teeth. Siegfried and Roy shine their teeth and upturn their collars. It is Beyond Belief at the New Frontier Hotel and Casino. Every day the father is up on the roof, or under it, laying the itchy insulation at various casinos. Circus Circus has a real circus with long legged showgirls, and also a buffet. The buffet is around the world travel. Here try this one, says the father, lifting a giant slice of pineapple with sticky ribs dripping in meat sweat. The mum sticks it into her mouth. Here try this one, says the mother, twirling giant noodles into a nest egg with hairy balls. The father sticks it into his mouth. Here try this one, says the father, piling the beef on a shrimp noodle waffle. Here try this one says the mother says the father, forever and ever. The mother crunches. The father crunches. The children crunch. The father fingers his molar, scraping and pinching the left over meatbits. Cheap eats, hide it in a napkin for later. Lucky the Clown has a giant lolly, it swirls and swirls, very high in the sky, you cannot eat it. Welcome to America.

Mr. America looks at the mum with three children, lets them into the apartment without a deposit. He brings the family coloured eggs, green, and no one knows where they come from. Mr America gives him a pair of metal roller skates, from an old tool shed. No one else has real metal roller skates. Everyone else has plastic. The United States of America is a land of plastic. They invented Tupperware. A soda pop. You twist the top, plastic. Handles, knobs, televisions, dishes, drapes and bathtubs: plastic. A house in Disneyland: plastic. All-American gum: plastic. Cowboy boots: plastic. Glitter: plastic. Stickers on the bananas: plastic. At the park the plastic swings swing higher. Slick riders slice around the sandpit on a knife's edge. The weary birds suck the gutter. Look in the bushes. A bounty of cowboy boots. They are made of plastic. Now you've got to ask yourself one question. Do you feel lucky? If you wanna guarantee, buy a toaster.

Sitting on the boxes, in the new empty apartment, he has his first McMuffin. He has the egg & the mum has the sausage, steamy soft, they swap halfway through. The father, after a day of laying insulation in casinos, comes to collect him. No kisses, you are too old for kisses now. The brown van is full of folders and parts, the new father always itchy, he is learning the new trade of air conditioning technician. In the middle of Arville Apartments, a swimming pool, chlorine, dry heat, the hot potato footpath. Next to the apartments, a patch of desert, he rides there, with his brother on the handlebars, stopping to lift rocks and catch lizards, horny toads, the gold standard. His brother Aaron, 8 years his junior, his only real friend in America, they lift rocks in the desert to build their muscles, scrape some change together for a shared sundae from McDonald's, made with fudge, or something like it, taking turns to scrape the fudge, with a wooden spoon, from the plastic ridges. In the swimming pool, diving for pennies, or Marco Polo, another kind of mission.

Pat, his first close friend. They watch the Harlem Globetrotters on his small television. His daily dinner, McDonalds, two cheeseburgers, with the sweet pickles, the bun plastered in ketchup, for extra nutrients.

During recess, sometimes kickball, with a big blue ball, or baseball, standing in right field, looking at the sky, he likes to oil the mitt. He prefers the soft balls over the hard balls. Or nerf football, with the flags tucked in his sides. Sometimes alone, under a tree, with *A Wrinkle in Time* or *My Brother Sam is Dead*. Exotic popular, on account of his accent, but mostly wanting to become invisible. Everyone pairing off, with a boyfriend or girlfriend, holding hands, briefly, on the playground, for one week. The break-ups and repairing happening quickly, a children's game of serial monogamy. Would you like to go out, play four-square, press our blubbery lips together behind the prefab, or there, in the corner, with the lights out, in the teacher's closet, 1 minute in heaven.

Everyone spins on cardboard, moonwalks, tries to move like a robot. When he spins the bottle it lands on a girl with the biggest bangs. Her nickname is bubblicious, big red bubbles, watermelon flavour. Her parents are dealers, card dealers. She curls her finger, wants to French kiss him, on account of his exotic accent, but he refuses, cites his new religion, and Jesus. Sometimes they trot to the 7-Eleven for slurpies, also Now-N-Laters, sometimes after Light as a Feather Stiff as a Board, or Kick the Can. He likes the chewy Now-N- Laters, you taste them now, and also later.

Have you done it, asks Pat, pointing back to the young

lovers. Older and wiser, he lets out a laugh, says you have to practice, maybe with a pillow, it gets better. The girl emerges with a glowing chin and the boy is all smiles. He hops over, does he want to come inside, watch a movie. The apartment is very tidy, everything in order, and in the corner, a whole shelf of movies, which one does he want, he lets her decide. *Pretty in Pink*, a classic, she says, scoots closer and puts her hand beside him. The movie finishes, and they move to her room, with all the posters, Debbie Gibson, "Out of the Blue," Only in My Dreams." A wooden box full of sparkles, scrunchies, ribbons and wristbands, very puffy pillows, another world. They sit on her bed, listen to cassettes from her boombox, and most especially Tiffany, "I Think We're Alone Now." That's when he feels it, the song is speaking to them. Do you mind if I hold your hand, she laughs, grabs his hand, and then a kiss, on the lips, a lingering peck, and then the hug, he wants it closer, a bearhug, a human body. It is sealed, they are boyfriend and girlfriend, and at the sandlot they hold hands.

The mum approaches the ice cream man and asks for a poke, waves a dollar in his face. No ma'am, he says, but the mum is persistent. A poke a poke a poke, she says, waving the dollar. They don't sell pokes in this country. During the Saturday morning marathon, the bishop calls and the mum, out of breath, says she is making meatloaf, a new delicacy. The bishop ends the call abruptly. He thought she was making love. He practices the American intonations, rising and falling, with his mouth, at night, in his room.

He walks past the crack houses & deflated kiddy pools & scrap metal cars. In the distance a Dairy Queen glows, the chairs bright red, plastic & hard. A woman is staring, she sips the cigarette and taps the ash, sips the cigarette and taps the ash. In North Las Vegas, Sades street, a HUD house. The boards off the windows, no deposit, sweat equity, their first house.

The boy, from Northern Ireland, is behind, and more immediately telling lies, an Irish ninja in hiding, someone might test him, says the teacher. One day, the boy from Northern Ireland is tested, but not terribly, a ninja performs a flying sidekick, under the basketball net, & he cannot top it. In the circle, the television is rolled in and they sit down to watch it. The Challenger explodes and everyone is quiet. Shortly after, the jokes. What colour were the teacher's eyes? Blue. One blew this way and the other the other way. From numbers to letters to living creatures. A circus bell of dead stars.

Read all the books and learn the lingo. Line up your gig line. Twirl the guns and straighten your spine. Line up on the grass and measure the space. You have a good mind when you're out of it. Do you have any wrinkles? A dark star passes through. The trees become thicker and thicker. The petals drip purple paint in the moonlight. It is a chemical explosion, but not the chemical explosion. Moving down the hillsides into the dank forest, swinging the scents on the end of a chain, back and forth, back and forth. The spirit is willing, they chant, whipping their back with leather and spikes. Someone is bone cracked on the rack. Someone is suspended above the Judas chair with olive oil on their anus. Steaming flesh on an iron maiden, boiling flesh on the brazen bull, the pear of anguish. Brown rats in the stomach, red ants in the orifices. A woman approaches, flesh of marble and a mass of white hair, orbs of white light in her hands. The thunder growls around her. You have to follow the elemental urges, she says. The ground cracks and you sink into the fatty folds. The light disappears into a thousand eyes.

He has the suck and cut, the suck & cut is not pulling hair, but almost. His hair has whole chunks missing. He adds some gel, makes it spiky, a little peach fuzz, a whole jar of chunky peanut butter in the blender. The chunks are hunky, a hunk is a large piece of something broken off from an even larger piece, & that piece is broken from an even larger piece, & that piece is broken from an even larger piece, & that piece is broken from an even larger piece. At the centre of the largest of the largest piece, there is nothing. Then the nothing breaks off, another hunk. We ride one hunk hoping for another hunk. The hunk is one of many hunks, and so on infinitum. Who can resist the hunk?

You need these, says the face doctor. He swallows birth control & splashes Sea Breeze. Scrubbing the inside, and also the outside, he is never clean enough. His right eye is moving further and further away from his left eye. His glasses get thicker and thicker & the mum pays extra to grind them down. On Sundays on the way to church in the back of the van they give massages, a foot rub, plus extras. They listen to Afterglow, to bring back the holy ghost, but sometimes they listen to Phil Collins *One More Night*. He leans over wads of bread and little plastic cups of water. This is called blessing the sacrament. In the bishop's office it is confession, you have to keep the blood away from your face, the blood to your face is a dead giveaway. He retreats to his cave and turns the milk pink.

A reclining beach chair with hot colourful slats for the water to drip through. A stud muffin skims across the water, a big hairy chest, neon orange glow trunks, up and down, arms behind his head. Between the Sahara and El Rancho, the turbines create the waves. Signature thrill rides. Hormones and wave pools. Ideal for hot weather. Hot dogs, chlorine, foot fungus. Hits of the 80's. Red lifeguards in tight trunks. Face firsters & fat tourists. The lazy river. They stamp your hand with the time. The countdown clock is at the top of the Sahara. King of the hill is a big bouncy with water slipping down it. There is a monster on the horizon. It is 76 feet. Can you climb it? A dive bomber. Lean over the edge and cross your arms, also your legs. Skim across the water. You always get crack checked. Your very own wedgie. His brother is 6 and he is 14. He holds his brother close to him. His sister at 4, white cream on shoulders and nose, a floppy hat. The mum in the slat chair. The dad, hairy, on the tubes. Everyone screams for ice cream.

Some shopkeepers, relatives from Portadown, come to visit. The parents blow up a kiddy pool and the shopkeepers keep their feet there, smoking and drinking, an American holiday. They take the bunk beds and he sleeps on the army cot. In JrROTC, with the lights out watching movies about MIGS and Russians. At night, after the shopkeepers have gone back to the home country, on the top bunk. On the floor, with a stopwatch to test his endurance for future partners, he goes there, with his hand, and rubs it, something warm slides out of him, milky water, 1%, not the full cream, he doesn't know what has happened, but also, he doesn't feel guilty. Under the bleachers the penis is warm and rubbery, he takes a drop on his pinkie, it is not brie. He feels it grow warm in his hands, & then the warm puddle, very comforting.

It's close to Christmas, a white turtleneck and thin gold chain, if you can afford it. At the entrance they take out their blue tickets, signed by the bishop, and then the final touches with the mirror. His hair a frosted waterfall and Doug sticking straight up. They are very different, but also similar, on account of the Bugle Boys, rolled tight at the bottom, but never more than two rolls. The DJ plays "Mamma Said Knock You Out." No, it's not time for the running man, it is also not time for the stomp and finger clicks and slaps. Bounce around with it, in your bones, let them see you have it in your bones. He bounces too much, becomes sweaty, it is almost in his bones but then again not quite in his bones. He needs more time for the bones. "Forever Young," a slow dance. He waits too long. Doug is bear hugging and he is watching. It is easy to become a wallflower. Do not become a wallflower.

After school, some string and tin cans. You wrap the string around the cans, from one side of the street to another, you hook the car, it becomes a clunker, rattles down the street. One day the police stop them, what are you doing. They don't answer. I was young too, says the policeman, you can tell me. They tell him and he asks what they are doing in the neighbourhood, it is not safe there. He points down the road, we live there, on the border of drive-bys and tinted windows. The policeman lets them off with a warning. They move to another street, string the cans, wait. They hook a brown boat car, from the 70s, half rusted, and it stops, then swings around, it really is an old clunker. Santa gets out with a busted balloon face, it wasn't me it was him, says Martin. The Santa fingers his chest for emphasis, then swinging fists. The voices say curl into a ball, no broken bones, some bruises, taking the lumps.

He tries the black, a bit Mod, and feels good about it, but not the turtleneck, too suffocating. He likes it loose, a neon green shirt, black boots. A runner, thick thighs and triangle calves. Shaving and growing, shaving and growing. His head shaved on the sides and tapered at the back, hairsprayed up and to the left at the front, not tight, a little floppy, the hairspray makes it choppy. Shaving and growing, shaving and growing. Long sideburns, very fashionable, except one side uneven, the left side bushy and the right side skinny. Shaving and growing, shaving and growing. Later, his hair parted in the middle, falling down, a fountain, but not even. Before the church dances, his mum curls it, with a curling iron, blow dries with mousse, a big puffy quiff. Shaving and growing, shaving and growing.

A man with the same name as his father flies a police helicopter. He climbs into the cockpit. Puts on the headset. How does it feel with the chopper chopping? It is good vibrations. Hardbacks, under his armpits, all his novels are war books, creased at the edges. He spills the lingo. Five klicks, two klicks, a hootch in the jungle. Now with an American accent, he is trying to become something different. He grabs the joystick, drops bombs over deserts. *Iron Eagle* is his favourite. They rescue the father from an unnamed Middle Eastern dictator. Pull the joystick down but don´t forget to tap the A to lift your landing gear. When turning, don´t spin. Don't fly too close to the ground. There are so many buttons. They are all blinking. Are you gonna drop the bomb or not? Heaven can wait. They are watching the skies. He is leaning into the future, his blond mop tousled. Life is a short trip living in a sandpit.

Everyday Mormon seminary, and afterwards, on the walk to the high school, they stop off at the donut shop, an old fashioned, cakey and heavy. One morning he grabs Chad, by the collar, against the wall, and then down the hallway towards the toilets. *Don't put your bag on top of mine.* All the other members, shocked at his actions, pull them apart. When you arrive late to the party, there is no place to hide your coat. Do you have the reign on your wild horses? Over the hill is a different country not much different from the first one and also strangely, different. When you arrive at your destination, it is never when you expect it.

Choose:
A) Scorpions locked in mortal combat
B) The praying mantis
C) The ecstasies of oysters

There are many kinds of fairies and this is one of them. They may float or appear to float. They cry like a cat in heat. Their clothing torn and tattered. Their spirit long and pale. The Banshee is chaos. It is not bound by oceans. You can send out all the NOT Banshee energy you want, the Banshee will still come. It is better to admit the Banshee exists, & then forget about it. If you are skilled there are many things you can do with a Banshee. The most effective, and perhaps easiest, is to never see a Banshee. Do not learn of Banshees. Never look at a picture of a Banshee. Do not engage or participate in any way in the telling of Banshees. The Banshee can steal some of your life force. Sometimes for a long time, sometimes a short time, sometimes forever. If forever exists, you are called the walking dead. Babies, between worlds, are easier to snatch. You can be marked by a Banshee when you are born. An offering to be taken later.

They keep a year's worth of canned goods in the basement. The mum turns on the radio and walks like an Egyptian, with her hands. At the dinner party, homemade Cornish pasties. Sherry and her boyfriend are dealers. The mum whispers to another woman, do you know why her nails are so long? No, says the other woman, crouched under the table with the crumbs. Cocaine whispers the mum. The boyfriend fans the cards, slicked hair and white jacket, Miami Vice. Eggs and brains in frying pans. Nancy Reagan with lollipops. Sherry's red nails disappear, one by one. Press ons, says the mum.

On the wall at home it is the last days, a woman's place is in the home, breast is best, says the current prophet. Knock knock, ring ring, everyone wants the money. Church donations. Hand me downs. More breakdowns, seven of her own and six others every morning, yapping babies, cooking & cleaning & handouts from the bishop. The mum, a hot balloon, wants to fly away. Her last nerve every morning and evening. At the drive thru at Wendy's, they make them square, deluxe, the ketchup thicker than McDonalds. At the drive thru at Carl's Jr., buttermilk dip and fried zucchini. The cravings, another sibling. They are building a big family for the kingdom.

Jesus stands on a cloud, arms open, thousands of trumpets behind him, the second coming. Have you done everything correctly? On the free breakfast and lunch special, at the governor's academy for the gifted and talented, everyone is low income, a ticket out, education. He is ranked 8 out of 996 students. Letters & medals & all-states. He gets 100% attendance at church, at seminary, at school, also martial arts, boy scouts, cross country, paper route, straight A's & other various activities. He steams the buns at Burger King and sizzles the dishes at Sizzler. He mows the lawn, changes the nappies, and rocks the babies. He prays 150 prayers per day, also hand washing, 45 times per day. But mostly, lately, a hankering for secret messages. He listens to the dictations.

It's a Thursday, a track meet, also inspections, you have to line up your gig line, you have to wear the funny hat and itchy pants. He forgets his change of socks, he runs the 800, 1500,

3200 and the relay in his black military socks. During practice runs he wears a yellow jersey, nipples hard and salty, through the streets of North Las Vegas, sometimes the sad park, full of the homeless, with 10 min fartleks, rolling green hills, a little valley. Don't drag your feet. Don't drag your feet, says Mandy. Lift them, it's more efficient.

There is a movie about going back to the future and a movie about standing on a desk and saying oh captain my captain. There is a movie with a guy holding up his ghetto blaster to win the woman he loves. There is a movie that says, if you build it, he will come. They take turns digging into the tub of buttery popcorn. It starts off as a crotch adjustment, then the rubbing of jeans, then the hand down the jeans. At the library with the Russians, an invisible hand under the table, with the lights out, during JROTC, with the MiGs and the Russians, a red dawn. The cock has a clit and you rub it in circles.

Everything is glam rock, white gloves and ribbons, polka dots pin stripes & tousled hair, bracelets & black bandanas & black leather jackets & long pointy boots, Motley Crue forever. While running, the same uniform, yellow for practice, green for the real thing, a rock in the cheek to keep the moisture inside. Running in circles, past Golden Gloves, the men bending sheet metal, mixing cement, plastering the walls. The future, probably.

The girls are in the corner boxing. Someone socks someone. A poached egg, bleeding. She says she likes them. The glossy magazine with body builders. He runs on ten gallons of horsepower, but only mentally, his arms are mostly wieners. He lifts and lifts but they barely get any bigger. But your legs, she says. The best muscles. His bottom half is the winner. He is trying to put his body together. He swallows his horse pills. There is a suction tube in the toilet with your name on it, says the mum. A magic jelly on his table. He hops over the whirlwinds, runs through the fields. Ice cream pies of America with seven layers. He licks around it, but has to crunch it. He cannot follow the proper instructions. You've got to raise your eyelids. At night the skies are more open.

Doug's mother sells burritos from a van to construction workers, they don't have to use their free lunch tickets in the cafeteria. He favours the breakfast burrito, with eggs and spices, & Mandy favours the chicken, they heat them up in the microwave. The dugout, a daily ritual, for make out sessions, sometimes no lunch, just the dugout, another hunger, many mouth fluids, then the dry cave, eventually a graduation to fence pressings, crotch fires.

At the zoo, animals pacing, animals slouching, a mustiness circles the air. At closing, deep kissing on park benches, chin dribbles. Mandy introduces him to the long jump, also the hurdles, also the pole vault. You stick your bendy pole and leap over. He runs the long distance. Here, says Mandy, a gift from a dead writer, Walt Whitman. He learns, temporarily, to love the body. The tongue, a little deeper, also, faster frictions, before the line was far away but now closer. He toes the line, doesn't cross it. They string the toilet paper around the trees, also the car tyres, an egged door, for the bishop's daughter. A good craic.

He swings the lamp of onionskins. He shoots the plastic cup full of water, sings to the mystery of its blood, dissolves the wad of wonder bread, sings to the mystery of its body. The bishop scans the room, picking up the red faces. The Sunday services, for three hours, the Wednesday services, for two hours, the various youth gatherings. He tries to make eye contact, without warming up his face. He thinks angels and golden trumpets. He gives himself the shivers, freezing waters, tries to cool his face. Sometimes, although not often, the occasional hum, Abide with Me, Till we Meet Again.

At the assembly, Mr. Williams re-enacts a drug shooting. I had more power between my legs than any of your pee-shooters. He grabs at the space between his legs. A former fighter pilot, he has been sent to recruit gang bangers. Some of the runners are homeless, some are working two or three jobs, everyone wants a scholarship, another future, there are not many choices, the cards are stacked, sometimes no basics. He rides in the van with cold cuts and lettuce. At the shop, picking up honey snacks and water, everyone stops and stares.

Terrell, his teammate and friend, pushes up his glasses, he whispers, they kill black people here. He feels his whiteness. He keeps his head down. Before the gun, the anticipation, after the gun, shoved to the back of the pack. You have to keep pushing forward.

The biology teacher draws organs skins and bones with both hands on the chalkboard, then he signs his name with both hands, at the same time, one hand going one way and the other hand going the other way, this is called bimanual simultaneous handwriting. He is very clever. His pants are baggy & he pulls the chalk from his back pocket, there are so many colours for all the organs, all the skins, & also all the bones. Now your turn, he says. They pull out their colouring pencils, begin colouring the organs, & also the skins, & also the bones. One day he brings the flies, very tiny. They come to the front for a small vial of flies. You have to get them to mate, he says. Each new fly is worth 10 points. Keep them warm, give them sugar and love, they live on sugar and love, he says. He takes his flies home, sleeps with his flies, wraps them in a warm blanket, sings to them, tells them stories, lots of love, but his flies do not mate. They are dead flies. He forgot the sugar, zero points. He meets Jay. All my flies are dead, he says. I forgot the sugar. Jay has lots of sugar. & now lots of flies. Can I borrow some flies, he asks? No, says Jay, but you keep some flies, I don't want them back. He borrows 10 flies from Jay. 100 points. A+.

Rebecca compliments him, his stylish clothing, a grey jacket, half cut above the belt, too small, second hand, a white shirt made of rayon, his skinny tie with paint splotched art, very eighties. He looks at her, powerful curls with hot braces, floral dress and floral fragrances. At the dance he wears the same outfit but cannot find Rebecca, probably dancing with a gentleman, the son of a bishop, higher up the ladder, not a lower class convert. He tries to keep his thoughts pure. In the corner, near the cookies, a group of girls with modest lipstick and plucked eyebrows, little triangles on the pocket of their bums, Guess jeans. He tries to keep his thoughts pure. He moves towards one, straggling against the sidelines, all her friends slow dancing. Maybe there's a chance, eye contact, any interest, she glances and turns away quickly, no interest or coy gestures. He steps back against the wall. He tries to keep his thoughts pure. A few songs later, in the corner, alone again. Do not look, hum the hymns, think of her spirit, away and towards, away and towards, something to strive for. He tries to keep his thoughts pure.

They pile into The Revolver, hairy legs and ribbons. He is a bent banana. At the library, the future kingdoms are before him. *Battlestar Galactica*. An array of ragtag spaceships. Blood and chrome. He strolls into the garden with a fruit rollup, rolls it back and forth on his tongue. They whisper from the branches. You must wear the green apron. Did the serpent tempt you? Do you want to get married for eternity? Where is planet kolob. He doesn't know what to do about it. The lost tribe of Israel is trying to find home planet. The Cylons are resurrecting their memories. They are going to take over. He feels the warrior spirit. I am nothing. I know I am nothing. Realistic daydreaming subconscious desires. There are so many choices. At the end of the lane there is an ocean and you can step into it.

In the final year of high school, he leaves Vegas, a rural life after everything. The father wants chickens, there is no room for chickens says the mother. They acquire chickens. And also, temporarily, a borrowed horse. The bishop's wife, across from them, has many peaches. The doctor, across and up, an open swimming pool. He mows the peaches and picks the pecans, scoops the dried dung and burns the rubbish. He watches the crawdads crawl through the ditches and listens to Nine Inch Nails. The town, named after a storm, is small. Farmers, mostly church members, also cowboys, some escapees from the city. Nearby, Zion, red rocks forever. A small group of white supremacists claim a white rock in Zion. They have shaved heads, black boots, a swastika. The patriarchs and matriarchs do not approve, they disapprove passively. On the weekends, the radical youth tip the cows. They are half asleep on their feet, but they do not fall. They are too heavy.

They move their tongues, twist their nipples, suck their

necks, then back to the mouth, twisting and turning, swapping saliva. This goes on for some time. Their mouth is a dry cave. A squirt, from the front seat, Mountain Dew, 62oz, more saliva. They move to the horizontal positions. He thinks future wife, going the distance. Levi loving, rubbing and rubbing, a small fire, and then the gushing. They keep their holes covered. Everyone returns to their respective vehicles. It is 3AM, back through the dust bowl, out into the fields, Jay idles the car into the dirt driveway. It is a hot summer night, they don't need a blanket, they sleep on the trampoline. Up and at 'em boys. It's Jay's father. He checks his watch. It is 6AM. You never know, sometimes it is a surprise, but less and less a surprise, when you spend the night you work in the morning. Where were you, asks Jay's father. We got stuck at the lake, says Jay. Until 4AM, asks his father. Yep, says Jay. Up the planks with the wheelbarrow, mixing the cement, the father examines his hands. Your hands are still soft, he says. He takes off the gloves, runs with the wheelbarrow, his hands start to bleed. Good, says the father, now you can get the callus. Jay sticks out his hand, it is all callus. I think he knows, says Jay. Don't tell him, he says. I didn't, says Jay. At the end of the day he runs 6 miles, behind the truck, to Jay's house. They eat cows potatoes and vegetables. In the evening the shovels. Keep digging boys, says Jay's father. Their arms are burning, and then he feels it, something else. When he relieves himself, he sees it, a giant blister. He doesn't want to pop it but maybe he should pop it. It is full of blood, what should he do with it, it is larger and larger, with a hot pin or just his fingers, he doesn't want to touch it. He keeps digging. Eventually they have created it, a large hole. They read the words of Jesus, and then the song. The wise man built his house upon the rocks, his house among the rocks, his house among the rocks. The foolish man built his house upon the sand, house upon the sand, house upon the sand. What do you believe? That was the central question. And what if you couldn't answer, you were supposed to be firm, a rock. He was not a rock but for a while he pretended he was the rock. A rock is fast vibrating energy, solid, water flows slowly, breaks down the rock.

His father peers into it, there is something there, maybe a sound, is it growling. The lights flicker, it is the differential says the father, he flips the switch and it comes back. You can't run the kettle with the iron, or the blow dryer with the toaster, the oven cannot run with the hob. You have to find the right combination. There is scratching behind the wall, probably mice, maybe rats, a whole family, the mother wants them gone. They arrive with tool belts, lay down the traps but nothing becomes trapped there. A little later, when no one is looking, his mother and father asleep snoring, he squeezes inside, there are chips on the floor, something gnawed, something taken, old wooden shavings. He moves a little further.

There is a small room with a small television, an iron in the corner, the kettle is on the hob. The living room is decorated, beavers on the walls, their great teeth gnawing, welcome they say. There is a polished oyster on the table. Babylon Babylon Babylon. A boy without a face, winds from outer space, the tides of indifference.

They touch bums in his bunk bed. The dad opens the door and creases his forehead. Later in the garden, the tongue, more bums, she cartwheels. In the evening they watch *Anne of Green Gables*. Anne is very sensitive about the colour of her hair, she exhibits great interest in everything romantic. Later, with Melissa's mother, he eats his one and only five course meal. They drink Martinelli and in between each course a spoonful of sherbet to cleanse their palate. My palette is limited, he thinks. He watches the crawdads, mows peaches into patches of grass, ties a red bandanna around his head & runs through the desert. There are many things in the desert such as rattlesnakes barns horses and country songs. Her mother pulls back the covering, the water bubbles, warm. Be careful of his back, whispers the mother, you can't give a man a backrub without exciting his baser natures. They ride the bubbles. His first love, the porcelain, what it does to him, her innocence. She thinks he is almost a jock, but he is only cross country, long distance. *Far and Away*. He is the Irish boxer and she is Nicole Kidman. His first love, the green eyes of the sea, a reminder of his home country, she is not a tanned American. They hike in the mountains, the pure streams. It never happens.

At Southern Utah University one of his roommates is South Korean. Joo-geen-dah is a sign of hotness. It means I want to kill you. His desk light shines into the morning. They forgot to flush the condom. He stacks the cans of Dinty Moore in his closet. He doesn't want anyone to eat them. It is your turn to wash the dishes. They are stacked high to the heavens. He keeps his own plate in the closet. He is not washing them. But didn't you use any of them. He is on a different system.

Back home for Christmas, there are rumours, goat worshipers, you have to be ready, they say. Doug sharpens his stick and then he sharpens his own. Cow skulls and gritty whispers, they are getting closer and closer, down the left side, a chill, then it slips down the right, from crown to toe. Near the H, a burnt-out fire, campers or goat worshipers, it is hard to tell.

In the park gazebo, he reads his papers, his true mission. Malissa Wads is disappointed, another strike against him, he is not going to Asia or South America, or some exotic location, he is only going to Idaho. He tries to see the connection. He came from Irish spuds and now, here in America, American spuds, but he also feels it, not special.

For a brief time, hair fountained, from the middle, uneven, shaving it was easy, a bowling ball, says the mum, parting on the left and dripping to the right, a good look for the mission. They buy suits, from Men's Warehouse, 2 for 1, one black and one blue, also cornflower ties. At his farewell they sing God Be With You. His friend John Atencio sits in the overflow, on the fold out chairs, a hard rock drummer with long black hair. Not a member, everyone stares at him. Also a few friends from Vegas, a Vegas Mob rapper and a future Marine, rough around the edges, but with short hair, less stares. The hugs and tears, a great honour, he is going on the mission.

In Boise Idaho, at 5AM every morning, The Missionary Guide. BRT means build relationships of trust. Families are forever. Colour flow charts and projectors, but now VHS movies to stir the emotions. Junior companion, senior companion, district leader, zone leader, assistant to the president, another ladder, if you get to the top you can ride the pink Cadillac. He rides a stump jumper. Every month a business spirit meeting. The wife of the mission president, a blond bombshell virgin mother, tells everyone to throw out their sponges, that's where the germs hide. They have to remember their sponges. The president is a multi-million-dollar winner. Up wins, says the president, with his thumb up. Everyone chants up wins with their thumb up. Down loses says the president. Everyone chants down loses with their thumb down. Then he shows them the pie charts, more baptisms, they have to stay ahead of the competition.

At Christmas, he buys a whole honey glazed ham with his monthly allowance, 200 dollars per month, a donation from the wealthier members, since his parents can't afford it, it is enough, since all the members feed them. The honey ham, it is an extra, some kind of indulgence. His companion agrees, food to fill the sad hungers, but they can't finish it, the ham too big, their eyes got away from them, their stomach rebelling, and after three weeks into the rubbish. P Day, every Monday, a half day to hand write letters to family, do the laundry, starch the shirts, pick up the groceries. Most of the missionaries play basketball, but he reads the books, non-approved, spells & whispers.

It starts with his second companion, frail, from Iowa, his first is a violin player from Virginia, a senior companion, but the second, a junior. In the middle of winter, he keeps the window open. We have to toughen up, he says. Also, bicycling uphill, at this time, also, spilling words in half sleep, a release valve. He breaks his toe on the third. The fourth is a Texan, mighty handsome, he is on the last leg of his mission, matching perms from the hairdresser. The fifth is riddled, ropes around the hands and bedposts for the prevention of nocturnal emissions, in the toilet, the door cracked to keep check on accidental rubbings, everything confessed to the president. The zone leader is a Danish viking, his favourite, they shave their initials into each other's crotch hair. Also, on a dare for free pizza, grape juice down the butt crack, caught, and drank later. The sixth, who knows, but the last is Swedish, pseudo intellectual. Here, he says, you can have them, his sacred garments, he wants to leave the mission. Do we burn them, he asks, the official report says we have to burn them? No don't burn them, says the Swedish companion, he saves them for later. The mission president needs a reason, no major infractions or transgressions, two sessions with the church psychologist. He says he wants to seek truth like a man whose hair is on fire seeks a pond, he stole it from Joseph Campbell, a minor infraction, it wasn't approved reading. Don't reveal the handshakes, says the church psychologist, put on your sacred garments, the devils are coming.

His father, when he picks him up from the airport, shakes his hand, an honourable mission, even though it ended early. In the town, lots of whispers. Did he reveal the handshakes, everyone stares at his family. His father on top of him, his younger brother on his father's back, his younger sister also, the great pile up. He feels his father's heartbeat, the closest he has felt to him, it is beating too fast, he doesn't want him to die. He lets him punch him, they are not hard punches, he doesn't mean it. He emerges, no blood, nothing broken, he runs through the streets and into the desert, his mother yelling after him, afraid of the drama on account of the neigh-bours. The bishop's wife across the street with her bucket of peaches. He keeps running up and down the hills of the desert until his legs and chest are burning. He leans against the fence, next to the cows, is there something in the distance. Cows and more cows. The electric hum of fences.

At home it is Wheel of Fortune, but he loves Jeopardy, tries to guess the questions, also reads novels, but they are always middle class or higher. He needs other stories. Border crossings and immigrations. They try to squeeze it out of you. So many decorums. What would we do without them? Chaos, pure chaos, the source of life and creations. He keeps running.

Over the hills and through the bushes, cow skulls, plus a wooden sign, swinging in midnight wind. They climb among the Martian landscape, red rocks and scrub bushes. A large bird flies over. It's maybe an eagle, they say. Eagles are some of the largest birds. They are at the top of the food chain, with some species feeding on big prey, like monkeys and sloths. Eagles have amazing eyesight and can detect prey up to two miles away. They are also freedom. Do you feel it, they say. The wind is howling at the moon. They take some steps forward, there is already a nice circle from a previous fire, just a bit of twigs for the teepee & some matches. Just as it sparks, a miniature cyclone twirls through the ghost town. A small tribe of children blow a greenhorn. There is the sound of spurs in the distance. They look at him with their marble eyes. Closer and closer, the marbles of his childhood, how he would flick them and also the cats, slinking around him. Do you have your dusters, they ask. He feels the cowboy. Calm stoic and steady with his fingers hooked around his belt loops. Nope, he says. He scrubs the toilets, empties the ashtrays, sweeps the courtyard, adds up the ticket stubs.

Smiley face from many years of smiley face conditioning. How was your weekend, asks the manager. Could have been longer. In the toilet, the ridge of the palm with good friction, circles, good to keep a fresh batch he whispers. The smell of burning ants is about to leave. The inquire within is about to leave. The darkness of day is about to leave. I just wanted to be somebody is about to leave. Afraid so is about to leave. The eternal moment of now is about to leave. The holy ghost is about to leave. There is a picture on the wall, it is not Jesus, it is a glowing mythical creature, owl-like, white hairs cover its body. During the second coming its small claws reach out to grab him, its eyes glow. They are looking into him.

He sleeps on the top bunk and at exactly 4.30AM he wakes up and goes outside, the outside freezer is humming. He feels lots of people around him, it's my ancient ancestors he thinks, whataboutcha, he says. He reaches out his hands to try and touch them, there is nothing to touch, a sheepdog barks next door, more and more yappy. The whispers of the holy ghost, you have to get back inside, it says, they are coming for you. His body feels heavy, his feet stick to the dirt garden & the crawdads glow in the crick bed. He walks past the humming outdoor freezer and opens the backdoor. The screen door is heavy, he pries it open, slips inside. When he reaches the top bunk there is something on his chest, & then he feels something pounding on his legs, twisted faces. The nose is in the wrong place. They come and go. He tries to shift his weight, stuck. Then he hears it, a voice from the corner of the room, near the ceiling. Don't drown, it says. It is maybe a sign he thinks. Eventually he falls asleep.

He is moving further and further. He thinks about his feelings, they are there, he doesn't know where, he tries to find them, drag them out of the dark into the light, he is constipated. He sits on the couch, places his head between his knees waiting, do they already exist, or do you build them. Maybe he needs to get right with Jesus. He feels something, it is not Jesus.

A junior college dance, posing on haystacks, skinny French fries with dollops of ketchup. In the mountains they ride down the hill in plastic bathtubs, he cricks his neck, hot chocolate with marshmallows in the evening. Her mother gone from the house, and also her sister, it was safe, but don't move, she says. It doesn't count if you don't move. You are only docking. He slips it off, a bit tight, pulling on the crotch hairs, he flushes it down the toilet, but it keeps resurfacing. Get it out of here, she says. He takes it out the back, buries it.

The pigeons bloat their bellies.

A big wooden conference table full of twelve men, mid 60's to 70's.

Did you reveal the secret handshakes, they ask.

No, he says.

Good, they say.

Have you kept your body pure, they ask.

He feels his face, there is hot blood running beneath it, heating up.

No, he says, trying to look square.

Hm, they say, scratching their chins and writing something on their yellow legal pads.

Did the woman tempt you, they ask.

We were in a cave, he says.

Was she on top or were you on top, they ask.

I was on top, he says.

Did you ejaculate, they ask.

No, he says, I didn't do it all the way.

Good, they say.

Did anyone have an orgasm, asks the oldest man.

No, he says.

So no pregnancy, they ask.

No pregnancy, he says.

Is she a member or non member, they ask.

Non member, he says.

These things can happen, they say.

The devil will try many tactics, they say.

It is good you have come forward, they say.

We have faith you can come back to the light, they say.

You cannot deny the light, they say.

We will need to pray on this, they say.

He waits outside the room on a plastic green chair, he scratches his head, & also his elbow. I have to get rid of the demons, how do I get rid of the demons, he whispers. When they call him back in they give him sympathy smiles and nod their heads.

Please sit down, they say.

The eldest member pulls out a long scroll.

We going to read the pronouncement, he says in a gravelly voice.

You are disfellowshipped.

The devils are coming, they say in unison.

As he is leaving, a lone voice, pleading, please put on your sacred underwear, it is your last chance. Yes, says another voice, faintly disappearing, you must wear the sacred underwear, it is for your own protection.

Just as he is leaving the room he turns back. They are all wearing sympathy smiles.

The demons hold a milk bowl of feathers. Blow they say. A flitter explodes into the sky. He cannot catch them. The morning sap. The porcelain sky. A string of runner beans

winds around his trousers. He snaps forward and the beans
scatter. The demons hold the door open, he cannot see. Drive,
they say. He backs out of the driveway, tries to go forward,
but it only goes backwards. He drives backwards down the
street, & then backwards onto the highway. There are many
cars, he cannot look over his shoulder, his neck isn't moving,
he hears the honks and feels the hot lights on his body. He
swerves off the highway & the tyres crackle and pop down a
dirt road. Where am I going and how did I get here is out of
the question.

He interviews at the local mercantile. The manager asks
about the secret handshakes, no, he keeps the handshakes in
his pocket. What about the prophet, no, he doesn't believe,
he just wants to stack and spray the veggies, sniff the milk
cartons, unload the crates into the secret chambers. The
manager disappears into the back room and then waddles
back. The matriarchs say they'll think on it, he says.

You can't put old wine into new wineskins. Jesus said it.
He scans the classifieds with ink-smudged fingers. There is
a job in a nearby city, a shoe salesman. He learns the shoe-
horns and soaks in the leathers, up and down the ladders.
He takes a cheeky peek to the children's department, tiny
t-shirts. Alejandra, three or maybe six years older, folds them
neatly, her fingernails red and sparkled. Should he ask her out.
There is the movie house next door, men with leather belts

and beepers, starched and tucked shirts, the women creamed and red lipped. No, not there. The Greek restaurant with the hippy waiter, and then, up on the mountain, near the D for Dixie, yoga from Yoga Magazine. They contort their bodies. The shakes are molten with chewy buttons. He hands her a skinny French fry, dips it in the shake, salty and sweet. They walk around sugar town & visit Ethan Allen. Look at this wardrobe, she says, it's heavy wood. He feels the wood. It's good wood, he says. There is a magic kingdom behind it, he thinks. And look, she says, a mirror. It is a very good mirror, he says. Gilded, he says. Gilded, she says. The couch is plush and he sinks into it. Elegant heels click all around them. A fairy tale castle in the distance. They are living in the gilded age, temporarily. They walk down main street, past the mall. Let's go inside, she says. The ads are beauty and gravity. Licitly split liquorice. Speedboat divas. His credit card overfloweth. The shops are black holes. There is so much gravity. You have to pull yourself together afterwards. Alejandra bends over the steering wheel and rains mascara. He is not enough for her. He sizes himself up in the mirror. Too skinny. His torso not equally balanced with his legs, almost 6 feet, but his trouser legs are only a 30. His waist was 32 but now 34, his nose, a ski slope, he can touch his tongue to it. A bigger firmer chest is not beyond impossible, he pushups and bench presses. It doesn't get bigger, but maybe a little firmer. Your nipples are smaller, she says. Is it a compliment? He is floating in space and she whispers into his space helmet. He pulls out his hand-made star chart. Here, he says, that's my planet. It is glowing green with pink dots.

He came home with a rabbit's foot and his mum was disappointed, shame shame shame. He refused to kill anything, neither the birds nor the rabbits, only the gutting of fish, only the chopped-up deer in the freezer, but he didn't kill it. His stepfather gave him the gun given to him by his father, a survival .22. Everything dismantled into the butt, easy to screw together. He hardly used it but he liked the simplicity. Also a sleeping bag, given to his step father by his father, from World War Two. A mummy, with the feathers sticking out of the hood, very itchy, it rubbed his ears.

He had forgotten extra socks, the snow came heavy. I'll run over the mountain, he said. There was nothing out there. We'll have to build a lean-to, or maybe an igloo. He was sweating, too warm, hypothermia. His father gave him chocolate. You have to increase your blood sugar. They slipped into the sleeping bag together. You have to increase your body heat. We'll have to signal a helicopter. The other boys prepared the smoke signals. There was no helicopter. The tyres spun in the snow. You can't do anything about it. The night comes loose in your hands.

The tinsel on the tree with extra sparkle. A few more and

everything comes into focus. At his cousin's house, he pockets a condom, tries one in the mirror. I don't want to see that, says his cousin. They smoke a few cigarettes in the graveyard, cover the smell with cheese and onion, or maybe prawn cocktail, before heading back to the Presbyterian parents

On New Year's Eve, they shave his head, a fresh skull, plus a piercing, a hoop in his left ear. He chooses a tattoo from the The Book of Kells, a half man half woman mermaid, left arm near the shoulder. They pub hop Stony Stratford. One beer then another and another. Don't give me a high five, says his cousin, it's not America. He says not to worry. He doesn't do high-fives, not even in America. At midnight everyone on the cobblestones, kissing strangers, he is feeling bohemian. By the end of the night he tries a joint, but only a little. He walks around the green puddle from his cousin's girlfriend, retires to the room with a little window overlooking the English garden. Queuing up for the new movie, there is a buzz around them, *Pulp Fiction*, he is feeling bohemian, smokes a cigarette. Don't slobber on it, she says. He has wet the filter. Everyone is bohemian. Castles in the air, a sensual calling, the bohemian is an outsider, at least temporarily, you can buy it but what if you don't have any money. How much does it cost for authentic bohemian? Sacrifice, purity, a burning mission, he is no longer religious. He is not gung-ho for material possessions. He is not an English dandy. He is not a Jesus bohemian. Who are your people? Are you a bohemian too?

She says she misses it, have you done it, she says. He has not done it. She pulls out the picture, her boyfriend in Australia. She pulls back her black hair, glosses her lips, slips back the picture. Don't look, she says. When he doesn't look, she slips into it, a thin black dress. Then down the stairs to the supermarket. Have you tried it, she says. He hasn't tried it, maybe he can try it, she says she tried it, and he pictures it, with her Australian boyfriend, a surfer, drinking beer on the beach and erasing their tan lines. Do you believe it, she says. He says he doesn't believe it. I believe it, she says, it's hard when you've already done it, you'll see when you miss it, she says. He almost misses it, even though he hasn't done it.

The problem is natural, how to have it, not fake it, even when you are reading from the screen. The screen is green, with tiny dots, it is hard to read, it would help to put your mouth over it. You have to make quota, after three hours without the quota, you are sent home early, without pay. Let's go, says the manager, a wind-up plastic doll. When he pounds the desks, a miniature gorilla. He imagines the manager holding the phone, naked, after a cold shower, the shrilled him, raisened, his skin chickened, forever and ever, but only for a moment, then it is back to *Sales for Dummies*. He reads snatches of Shakespeare between calls. The words, so foreign, far away, a different planet. Scroll down, click for rebuttal one, click for rebuttal two. There is the affirmation, if you are lucky. The closer seals the deal, tapes the end of the conversation, reads the final script. The voice of a hypnotist.

Jesus on the ceiling. The wet gush. They read his patriarchal blessing, feel the burning in their bosom, did they know each other in the pre-existence? She leans closer, reaching around and squeezing it, the bum. She leans closer, takes a drag, plants her lips there. They rub together, fully clothed. Sweat flakes off his eyebrows into white sand. In her room they try not to do it, think of Jesus, but they have already done it. Against the wall, under and over, carnal gymnastics, the full press. They have to try harder not to do it. The doing of it. It is hard to stop it. They walk across the street to the petrol station, a styrofoam cup, the oily black liquid topped up with creamy hot chocolate. It is the best combo, she says.

They put a towel on the floor to catch the drippings. He unzips the fly, the cock in his mouth, a fantasy favourite, around the manclit some dry skin, or something more, he is not sure, he keeps sucking, should he taste the cum, he has tasted his own, he keeps sucking. Tristan slides out of his mouth, lays down on the towel, slips out of his shirt. He slides in his penis and they face each other, some kisses, the stubble from someone else, a new feeling. Tristan's penis bounces on his stomach, he wants to grab it, suck it, medium sized and thick, a new feeling. He pulls out, cums on Tristan's penis, they rub together. Tristan gives him an anthology of Irish literature. They hide the chocolate under the pasta. He uncorks the cork. The swans flap their wings, jump the rapids.

He meets her for all-you-can eat. The pizza crust is really a cracker, not Italian, extra crispy, very thin, but also filling, three plates or more. I want it, she says. Are you sure, he asks, it is not worth it. She says it is worth it, something to wash it down. That's their big profit, he says. No, she says, she wants it. It's really a scam, he says, we shouldn't fall for it. No, she says, it doesn't matter, she wants it, something to wash it down. It is cheaper later, he says, around the corner. It is better later, he says, he read about it, not to drink while eating, much healthier. No, she says, I want it. Just pizza, water later, he says. No, she says, I want it, from the machine, not later from the corner. A Diet Coke, all you can drink, not a biggy, he was only trying to save money.

Her father talks about the physics of golf swings & his intentions, will he marry his daughter in the temple. At dinner he tells them he prefers the Dalai Lama to the prophet. I don't believe in special privileges, says the father. She is torn between them. Maybe he can return to it. He slips into the sacred garments, down to his knees and elbows, and then the big meeting, a celebration, via satellite, of the founding prophet. He walks out, he can't do it. You are not trying. They try not to make love. They make love. They try not to make love. They make love. At the wedding, the rake and shovel. An ancient kilt. Down the line, shaking hands, her uncle curses him.

Some of her family work for Marriott, so he gets a job there, making reservations at the call centre. They move to Layton, a small city. A few beers in the fridge for later, but not when her brother is coming to visit. The carpet is pulling away from the walls. Smiths is a short walk down the gravel driveway. The bus to the university, philosophy and English, a few hours of sleep, it is hard to keep the balance between full time work & study. Stephanie works for the recruiters in Salt Lake City. One of the recruiters, Emma, and her boyfriend Logan, invite them to their wedding. A woman priest, balloons in the air and dancing on the tables, a celebration without the weight of religion. There are other ways of living.

It is midnight. The searchlight beams straight up, into the sky, then it circles around. It is calling them. They buzz down the freeway. All the vehicles are larger and they are tiny. Do they dive defence or offence? They try not to get sandwiched. They follow the midnight beam to a car lot. The salesman is thick knuckled and golden. They test run a used convertible with the top down. Stephanie beams Julie Roberts and twirls her red spaghetti. He beams his chisel. They are rich, temporarily, and all-American. The salesman crunches the numbers. With their new jobs in telemarketing, plus their evening cleaning, they could make the payments, barely. They are in sync with the thrill of becoming different. Why does the heart thunder? How much do you have to do to die happy? He touches the triangle of hair on his dimple. Maybe they can clean more buildings on the weekends. There is little chance of winning more commission for selling Burpees. Their car is 50 miles per gallon and good economy. But it is only 49 horsepower. It is not American. They sit down in the diner to contemplate their future. Moons over my Hammy or the Grand Slam?

They bake the brownies, order a pizza, wait. I think I feel something, she says. Then nope, nothing. I think I feel something, says Andy, then nope, nothing. This goes on for some time. It's not really working. Then, suddenly, it is working. They crowd into the kitchen and devour the Cool Ranch. They all lean closer to look at each other's faces. This is a one-person kitchen, says Andy, everyone out. They spread around the small apartment. Lay down, close your eyes, when you wake up everything will be normal. Stephanie runs to the toilet and he follows her. I just want to feel normal, she says, over and over. Ride the waves, he says. I don't want them, she says, sticking her fingers down her throat. He flies over the swimming pool. His mouth is silent, he can't open it. He swims under the water, pulls the plug, but then remembers, the water is your unconscious, he better replug it. The plug has grown bigger, it won't fit. He pushes harder and harder. The water is draining, soon it will disappear. He has to plug it. What is he plugging?

They bloom there, among the cafes and live blues concerts, and for the first time local beers, no more Buds or Millers, the lush green of it, and yes the ocean closer. Andy follows them a year later with Modest Mouse. They hotbox the car. Sometimes hiking the foggy mountains, watching the whales migrate to Alaska. Sometimes cafes, art and aesthetics. Andy learns all the songs of Bob Dylan & applies for art history at Cambridge. The secret door, in Vancouver, from Mexico City to Paris, all in Vancouver, the various languages, something awakening, a North American Amsterdam. Secondhand t-shirts, hemp hats and necklaces, Schnapps from the Germans, local salmon sandwiches, potato burritos, silky rich coffee. Are you ready for a family, she asks. It has been five years. Maybe soon, he says. He is drowning in theories. He reaches out to touch them, the trees in the arboretum. The whales ride their whale-ways to Alaska. He attends his first concert. The singer wants to burn one down and they pass it around, thick as a newspaper. Two large men collapse in front of him. He can hear the singer, further and further away from him, a tin voice, and then the sound of his blood rushing, his heart beating faster and faster. There is a hole in his shoe from the dragging. When he opens his eyes, they ask him the problem. Some more, they say. It won't kill you. The best things can't be spoken.

He wants to wet his tongue with it, the slow dripping southern accent. He applies for the creative writing program. He wants to become something. On Carr Street they rent a house, two doors down from the director. Art as community, the best lesson, can you take something serious that doesn't make any money. Dante and Southern Gothic, the BBQs and hooch. Bluegrass, Coltrane, Doc Watson & Earl Scruggs. The annual Halloween gathering, a tradition for over thirty years. All the students and former students in the house dancing, on the porch with the beers, on the rocker with whiskey. More house parties, his teenage years at 30. The young and the restless. She works at a lab, some classes at the community college. She is feeling the nesting. They are different kind of people. She asks him to come to lunch, drive over to her workplace, but he cannot do it, the fears. She suggests a weekend trip, to the mountains, but he cannot do it, the fears. Balled up in the shower, the sobs. Zoloft and other experimental cocktails. PTSD and anxiety. When he is not teaching, he keeps the curtains closed, no phone or doorbell, too loud, upstairs in the room painted yellow, with the giant desk made by her father for his birthday, trying to write life changing poetry.

I wish you would slap me, tell me to shut up, she tells the marriage counsellor. What is the mission. Show some emotion, she says while poking him. Anger is from the devil.

He remains calm. Show some emotion, she says, again and again. He throws the Christmas tree across the room, punches a hole in the wall. OK you can stop showing emotions now, she says.

French Lunch, beer butt chicken, a hummock between the trees, grapes on the nipples. Something he always wanted, a more bohemian existence. One day, feeling something in the air, they stop cuddling and playing, they have to separate them in different rooms. Mona is anxious and needs medicine, but Iris shits behind the television for attention. Mona is plump with snaggletooth. Iris tortoise shell, very wiry. They visit the doctor. More medicine. Iris is running up the walls and Mona nestles. They cannot reconcile their differences. Do you have the right medicine? Transport the smells from one to the other. From Mona to Iris, a small blanket. From Iris to Mona, a sniffed finger. From childhood to late adolescence, curled in her jacket from the shelter, the electric buzz at their feet in winter. It isn't working. They cannot keep them together.

They come in small bags. You have to eat them all, says Lydia. They sit around the table. Ken tells them he is going to join the army, pay off his art degree loan via government forgiveness. Lydia tells them about the strippers, her friend's pre-nuptials, around the back, near the shed, the group blow-jobs. When they row out to the island, Stephanie and Catalina slap the oars with the water. We have to keep rowing, says

Lydia, we are almost there. On shore, they split into groups, the talkers and non-talkers. The non-talkers sit in the boat, half in and out of the water, half beached and half rocking. Do you see them, asks Ken. He says he sees them. All the body parts floating by them, breasts and cocks and cunts. Tigers eyes and water lilies. There are too many bits to describe.

Stephanie picks up a giant tortoise shell. It's prehistoric, says Lydia. They ramble through the bushes and emerge into a large clearing. The bark is crawling in fluorescent green insects, smaller than a penny. They lean in closer and watch them, but do not let them crawl on their hands. On the other side of the island, low tree branches, perfect for swinging and dropping. There is something hanging from the trees, small bits of metal, reflecting the sun. When they arrive there, they find them. Small machine tree sculptures.

Back at base camp, they fire up the BBQ as the sun is sinking. Retired senator houses in the distance. Into the town, later in the evening, they meet the thick fingered fisherman, mending the nets. Fish cakes in the bar, they neck a few beers. Lydia tells them they have entered it, another way of seeing. The next morning, the jellyfish, fluorescent, glow beneath them. Stephanie moves towards the water, fills her camel sack, tells everyone to sit upon the log before them. Then she baptises them, in the name of the mother goddess.

The painting, purchased at the beginning, in Utah, androgynous figures, in all white, alien and beautiful, emerging from the earth, the one in the middle, reaching up to the ball of yellow on the right, warmth and life. The ground a desert. It hung on their walls from Utah to Washington to North Carolina. Also the sculpture, a half circle. Married too early, his ex-wife almost 19 and he was 21, a half circle, before trying to complete their own circle. Know thyself? You have to go back to the beginning. The shiny heart of existence, absurdity and nothingness. Finally letting go, a relief, only to build it up back again. Not a life lived but a life living.

They have to find the spark again, where is the spark? Wild sex in the church, behind the crucifix, where they held the MFA thesis readings, also later, during an MFA party, in the parked car, pegging, the cock is too large, a butt plug, it stings, his spatial reasonings. Love and belonging, coming home, how long does it last. The traveling, not a place or destination, the momentum for something over the hill only to find another hill and a rock to roll, rarely looking back, taking account, rarely observing and accepting. The nothingness, pregnant with possibilities. Not nostalgia but the wake of a boat, still sailing, maybe for a little while or longer, before the swallowing, a sickness, but also a beauty, the pains and also the pleasures, another human being. You are not alone, real or imagined, caught up in the nets of nationalities religions and genders. Various distractions. The love, yes, a bridge. There was no telling for how long. A human warmth and connection. Destruction and creation. These are the days of our lives.

Greyhounds and boxers. A Danish pipe and bald head. Dan builds a wooden porch, with his bare hands. He builds a treehouse. Invites them for grits & sweet meats. The thick air of the summer, biscuits and white gravy. Tailgating at Clemson. Ribs in secret sauce. Combing the stacks of the university, ingesting everything, trying to find it, a new vision. The lush Spanish Moss. The mysteries of new insects.

In Philadelphia with white Russians. In Atlanta with southern text explosions. At Pete's Candy Store with air banjos. In DC verbs swarm the nouns. Window water baby moving. The spirit of creation. The lyrical sublime. He shows them his pinhole. Dark light projectors. A little hooch in the forest. They pull the daisies. Guided by voices. A beard of bees hangs from the trees.

When was life going to begin? Maybe it had begun already. The brains two circles, with one overlapping the other, the shared space shaded, a Venn diagram. Constantly changing. Hungry for new experiences, different parts of what if. Memories are snowflakes or at least overlapping. Or not quite. Downing our primal histories. The sink, baby blue, attracts soap scum. They take some pictures. Photography means writing with light. Are you going to squeeze the lemon?

He can finally see it. He is almost invisible. A layer of towels to cushion the thumping. Back in Utah, a family portrait. They are no longer smothering the enchiladas. They are riding the elliptical. The weight is dropping. The lights are blinking. The balls are spring loaded. Outside the window, an invisible orchard, the branches waving, budding cherries. In the mornings, the world tilting. An experimental cocktail. His scalp tingling. In the thickets, the meat is dripping. She leaves at Christmas. He moves into new time zones.

Wonderland

He ticks the boxes, sits near the conveyor belt, not spinning. He is gathering different lights from different countries. The blinking lights for food. The blinking lights for clothes. The blinking lights for schools. Small windows one after another, bathed in red lights. In the new flat, two rings for cooking, a tiny fridge, washer and small bed with a window. On his second day boiled caterpillar, meat on a stick, the palace of wisdom. The crowds become thicker and thicker. Blown with the wind, lost in the crowds. Don't panic, walk the streets. Moles with rubber hammers. Metal chopsticks. Sauce to knock your socks off. The spicy fermenting kimchi sits nicely in his tummy. The beer bubbles his head. His foot is asleep. A toothbrush later.

Faces are a main part of any application. They share shots of soju. Joe touches his dimple, leaning in closer, you have a good face, he says. I can recommend you for the opening. He's mostly clean shaven, a little shade beneath his chin line. He moves his smile lines. You should shave it, says Joe, pointing to his goatee. Maybe I can leave a triangle, he says. Better clean shaven if you want to make the impressions. Someone reads his face. A good face for Asia, innocent, non-scruffy. A baby face underneath him.

To rent a flat in the city you need key money. 5000 dollars. Impossible. They recommend a goshiwon, student housing, a small room with a bar above his head to hang his clothes.

Wonderland is losing face. He is leaving the gifted and talented, but not really. They call the recruiter. The recruiter is going to lose his bonus. You made a promise, he says. Wait another year, he says. Sorry, he says. You must, he says. He pays the 2000 dollar fine, back to zero with his savings, but worth the price of freedom. Wonderland is losing more face. Joe calls him, the boss above the boss, maybe a gangster, they can blacklist you. You have to come back, he says. I can help you later, he says. Bosses above the bosses above the bosses above the bosses, he says. Wonderland is losing more face. Joe calls him, late at night with the tiny television playing Japanese game shows. On a plank with a plunger, the walls sliding down and under. Inside a golden tomb, wrapped and sealed as a mummy. In a tank with giant spiders and other creepy crawlies. Things are getting dangerous. He feels anxiety. Late at night in his goshiwon red crosses light the night sky. Love hotels and brothels, a rest for your penis, discount electronics, various kinds of shopping. The people on the street, are they watching, how can you do anything. So much isolation. Where are friends in this equation.

A French man arrives from Africa. They walk the city. Lights buzz in the night & larvae boils on the streets. They eat fire chicken, sip Soju during San Gyup Sal. An owl eats the pussycat. A secret worm eats the owl. I can take all of you into my mouth. They open the door for morning glories. Heat comes from the floors.

Dust blows in from China and there are millions in masks. He searches for ham but only finds spam. Live animals crawl in the shops. A pillow by night and a sack by day. The petals begin to fall. He explains some things from his childhood, about kissing and rubbing. He was thick, he says, & we massaged each other in the back of the van, on the way to church. He cannot cry, but sometimes he whimpers. The dust is thick. it comes from the Gobi Desert.

They can't get out of bed except to eat Korean pizza with hot sauce. They like to wash by way of experiment. He shaves his pubic hair to get a better grip with his mouth. The temple is dripping with rain.

When spring comes, they pluck their eyebrows into twin hyphens. His soft face fucks his soft thoughts. They eat at the sushi bar. His cock grows against his leg. The light is slanted rain. What is a state of thought, he says. My state or yours. We can only guess.

In the communal showers they lose their thoughts. Don't

you love me baby? Tell me tell me true. They are wet and happy. Everybody wants to go to Japan, but everybody should just hold hands. Welcome to the Korean summer, eating bulgogi and bean sprouts, small pickles and quick sushi. Keep it neon. Keep it light. He buys a tiltable screen. Now I can look you in the eye.

In Osaka, they walk past the giant crab. We have to memorise this, he says. At the whisky bar they meet jovial Japanese gentlemen. A bowl of nuts on the table. One hand and then another, sometimes brushing. He loses him somewhere between the sinking lanterns. It is 2AM and a woman links his arm. In the small room Japanese women are singing karaoke. Two of them sit down beside him. They want him to order them a beer. Three Budweisers, and then two more. They keep sipping and spitting the beer under the table. They don't drink them. A curious custom. Two of them sing for him, in thick Japanese accents, with a mic and a small speaker. "My Heart Will Go On" by Celion Dion. His guide, an older lady in her late 60's, points to one of the singers. She smiles a lopsided smile, chipped teeth. You have whole night, she says. She slides closer to him, begins to sing more loudly. He waves his hand and shakes his head. The other lady sings more loudly. Just the bill, he says. They take his debit card from America. The paper comes and he signs for it. He walks down the stairs. He has to find the giant crab. A man runs past him in a well-fitted suit. As he reaches the bottom of the stairs, three more men come running. They catch up with the first man, pick up a bicycle, begin smashing. The Japanese mafia. He walks faster, finds the giant crab, moving in the brisk air. Shortly later, his hotel. A catnap. A few hours later he gathers his documents for the flight back to Korea. He finds the receipt. 1000 dollars. Five Budweisers and bad karaoke. He cannot go back there. He cannot contest it. The bank will not refund him. The services not listed, only the amount, 1000 dollars. No name for the establishment. He had signed for it.

He is feeling younger. In Itaewon, avoiding the American soldiers, and also the Russian mafia, on a dance floor with Brazilian models. Exotic cocktails and fancy clothing. Various feathers. They watch them from the sidelines. He wants to stay, but then, upon further inspection, mostly due to the loud music, he wants to leave. They have missed their transportation so it's the love motel. Much cheaper. He can afford it. The pillows are heart shaped and also the bed. Everything plush red. Just so you know, he says. Yes, he says. They cuddle to the sounds of the squeaking beds above and below them. Try to drown it with the sound of Korean game shows. In the morning, a mini hug, no kissing. They move to their prospective destinations. He isn't ready for anything serious. Alone and isolated, back at his goshiwon, his watches the Korean game shows. Snow blankets the windows. He moves the palm of his hand around his stomach in circles to try to dissipate the gas balls. But where are the gas balls. It is hard to locate their origin.

They sneak soju into the stadium, learn Korean baseball, watch the World Cup together and drink Guinness. Late sessions at Tin Pan 2, wandering the city during the dust storms from China. A trip to Busan, in the south, for the beach, and also Itaewon for Indian buffets. At the Korean health spas, a wooden pillow for you head. A bubble tea and a face lift. The warmth is beneath you.

The sun on their finches. The feathers in their cup. Love is a soggy look. Orange hair & cowboy boots. Hug me in the sunlight. The man on the left has more estrogen than the man on the right. I will masterfully perform a thin penetration. There are no tapeworms in the chamber pot. An evening performance of fruit sellers.

Doraji, doraji, doraji! I walk over the pass where balloon flowers bloom. It is a path that is familiar to me. Hey-ya, hey! An ya ha say yo. Reminds me of mother & twinkling boys. Hey-ya, hey! An ya ha say yo!

His garment of rice. His empire of folds. He barebacks a man from Texas with beautiful cheekbones. Dew drops itself into the stew. Crouching with Aphrodite. Here his trousers split. Here his sparrows split. Here his oceans split. Here!

At the end of the night, holding the phone to his left ear, he tells him he's eaten all the tenderloins

They reek of kimchi. A turtle pillows them. Ancient horses have crossed the bridge. In the goshiwon the room is £25 per week. The clothes hang above him.

They meet in a tunnel while snow licks their lashes.

They meet in a coffee shop.

Oh rejoice for the communal kitchen.

The lights of the night commute.

Mongolian mermaids throw their hooks into this soil. Hot and dry. Be fruitful & multiply.

Oh Rumi i i i i i i i i will not paint dream brothers, dream lovers.

Boys kiss boys in the shadows. Hug the stalls. Orange fish eggs & salmon slices, oh boy. A tonked up meathole. Cramping at the knee. Swamp grass. Yogi-YO! An allegory breaks in the mouth. The old wood sticks out from the newer handle. The neighbouring dust will have its way.

His address is 813 Dae Yang Nice, Gae Sang, Gye Yang, Incheon. Joe is a veteran of the gulf. Shane has a ponytail. Tim meets them on the roof and runs through the numbers. His ipod contains: Promising the Light. Ocean Breathes Salty. Naked As We Came. Kissing the Lipless. The King of Carrot Flowers. Somebody that I used to Know. Junkyard. Bird Stealing Bread. He's Simple He's Dumb. I Don't Blame You. Float On!

Greenline to Shinlim Station. Exit 3. Bus 5529. Date with B. 3:45PM at Gangnam Exit 1. Saturday 2PM Yeoksam 3. Blind date from Korean Friend Finder. 250 grams of meat. Must find hanging closet.

Into the world. Into the gold painted night sweats with Mr. Goar. He left his broken watch in Jakjeon but picked up a hipper one in Myeong Dong. DAE HA MIN GUK!

Sexing doubt the radio is a vibration from the underfloor. I'm drumpy, you're simple, I'm considering drinking your ass juice. Pain became a passage, a muppet. Do not, do not make, do not make me, make me wear flares. Spit cherry pits. Stick glass in tummy. Munch Rumi. Let us then mate.

Through the secret side door to save face. The office is light green with a fish tank, swimming and swimming, it is meant to be relaxing. He has the old bottle, an experimental cocktail, they mistranslate the label. He wants to jump out the window. He is getting fatter and fatter. Korean men are slimmer. He pinches his belly. He has to visit the trainer. He combs through his clothes, no no no, occasionally yes, it depends on the labels. They visit the special market. He feels special. 40 dollars for a t-shirt. Something from North America. He tries to trim his stomach. He is getting better and better. Can he become a new creature?

Your hair, he says, maybe blonder. He dyes it blonder, but still the stomach, a holdover from America. He has to become trimmer. 100 crunches. 200 crunches. 300 crunches. The personal trainer eggs him on with a weight ball. He is not losing weight, only gaining. It's the pills.

It is almost summer. A three-month holiday paid for by the university. Plus, a contract with a textbook company. He is climbing the ladder. His clothes are getting better, but his head is getting worse. He looks at the window. He looks at the window. Opens and closes it. He thinks about his divorce papers, newly signed, 10 years of marriage. He is only 32. There is still time. He uses all of his savings for an emergency ticket to Northern Ireland, back to where he started. A failed romantic.

Heaven is a stage. We are lost in the flexi glass with wet fingerprints. With our blood. With our native sparks. Buzzing around the mud pit, hacking ducks with a machete. He carried the river on his back. It broke into ten thousand splendids.

The bright green and orange parrots are outside his window. They are beautifully lost.

There are more things in a closed box than an open one.

Make haste yea gentlemen who ride across the seas.

His housemate awakens furniture that once slept.

Snail shells were once used as an allegory for both grave and resurrection.

Every morning he gives a thought to saint Robinson Crusoe.

Water Bugs float on the china plate.

Q: Was I in yr tummy when you were dancing?
A: No!
Q: Where was I?
A: Nowhere.
Q: Where is nowhere?

★

He is changing the weather in his brain. The ghosts of material things. A small lint free cloth, two coins, a small twig, and unresolved scum clog the washing machine. Fashion couples the living body to the inorganic one. It defends the rights of the corpse. Time is embedded in the spaces of things. A collective redemption of lost time. He is little red riding hood in a sea of lights. Who is the wolf? Litho Cardites are heart shells. Images set verbs in motion. The French proverb says if you steal an egg you steal an ox. Houses are made from liquor and saliva. What is the dreamlife of language? The wing is near the engine. Every land a jigsaw. Etwas schnell. Eat the snail. Listen to me. He needs a goading. Will you goad him? A tight squeeze of the lid doth not drive away wrath. Behold his face how it bores him. More and more went in and more and more came out. Folks pay a fortune for their lives.

They have blown up the herd, ground in the mad and let go, imposter, self-posture.

We are

hustled

into the

future

Confucian harmony -- between – what we have -- and what

we owe

a moving

back – below – a wandering – kingdom –

no name – but love

The Hanged Man

He interviews on the phone, the Callan method. Does he know gerunds. He knows gerunds. Congratulations. He books his ticket to Poland. In Rybnik it is zapiekanka, later, around the corner, Polish pizza, with real garlic dip, and then the mountain man, lard with salted bread and little dumplings with white curd cheese and potatoes. At the end of the first week, the dance club, a new wildness. They dance on the tables, a kiss around the corner.

I have to tell you something, she says.

A man is coming toward them.

She moves further away.

I am married, she says quickly, in an open relationship.

The man is standing next to them.

Take care of my wife, it's my only one, he says, laughing.

Later in the beer garden, am I a way to make your marriage stronger, do you get jealous of each other.

Yes, probably, she says.

During the summer, a week in London. He lays down in the damp parks. An English sandwich, with various spreads. The best, eggy mustard. He drinks a coffee, uses the toilet, some-one knocks on the door. This is not your private toilet. He has to squeeze quickly. Back in Poland, he visits the Katowice train station to check his email. Your contract is null and void due to gross misconduct. He writes back for an explanation. She pastes a link to his blog. It says one day he would like to leave Poland, maybe live in London, also he doesn't like teaching children. Back in the flat, bread mashed into the carpet, the butts overflowing the ashtrays, Trevor on a bender. Just talk to her, he says, smooth it over. The owner of the school leans into her chair. Do you have a cigarette, she asks. He gives her a cigarette. She ashes under the desk into the rubbish bin. What if the parents see it, she says. It was only the moment, he says. He cannot afford to move to London. He is going to stay in Poland. I can't trust you, she says, how can I trust you, she says. I can teach children, he says, but I prefer teaching older people. I can take it down, he says, it was only the moment. It's too late, she says. How can I trust you? He waits for his last paycheque. It never arrives.

He stays at a hotel for retired miners. In the morning, he meets a retired miner.

Tyskie, do you like, asks the retired miner.

He likes.

Others, more sullen, outside in the nearby beer garden, staring into their beers.

He walks with the retired miner, only a few words between them, some Polish and some English.

Next time I'll get it, he says.

The retired miner doesn't understand.

I pay, tomorrow, he says.

Nie nie, he says.

OK, he doesn't want the returned favour, a generous gesture, no strings, welcome to Poland, he says.

Every day, a few beers, or a dozen, and in the evening, with a towel over his shoulder, lining up for a shower, and always leaving the key at reception, a requirement, maybe just in case he lost it, or a signal he was out of the room, he doesn't know. They tell him it was a five-star hotel, under communism.

He finds a job in Zory and Jastrzębie-Zdrój, teaching English in the villages, the long bus rides, 300 dollars a month, but free housing with an old catholic lady, Miss Wróbel, a widow with an old-fashioned boyfriend, many crucifixes, flush the butts down the toilet.

It is summer and everyone licks the ice creams, very popular in Poland, down the streets, licking around and around, they are very good, refining his sensuality, the ice cream, but also the responsibilities, just around the corner, seeing the married woman, if she left her husband, a 13 year old daughter, plus the reliance, on language as well as money, lopsided, what could he provide.

After late night drinking with the married woman, back in his room, they try to be quiet, but Miss Wróbel opens the door, right when he is orgasming. She tells Aleksandra to leave, she doesn't trust her, she might steal something.

At Hotel Diament, in Jastrzębie-Zdrój, a place for Matura parties, but mostly empty, and downstairs a bowling alley, a shelf in his room for some bread, no fridge or kitchen, he mostly eats sandwiches, or canned food, some wodka.

She is moving to Krakow. She will divorce her husband. Does he want it. He doesn't want to repeat himself. Safety or adventure. You have to choose your suffering.

The book says Polish in 3 weeks. He learns various phrases, often of little or no use, at least practically, on a day to day level, such as wyglądasz jak zmokły szczur, part of the dialogue in a knajpa, a rainy day, the woman coming in wet, the man flirting, was it some kind of joke, but when would you say it, you look like a drowned rat. His first week in Poland in a knajpa, hungry but also thirsty, ordering a Tsykie, and then seeing them, hanging behind the bar, a bag of crisps (British) or chips (American), and having learned the word for chips (British) was frytki, he surmised, maybe, the chips were cipki, so he asked for two. The bartender, a woman, reddened, called someone from the back, and a large man, neckless and strong, loads of muscles, the Polish having the strongest men in Europe, the world champions of strong men, appeared in front and pointed to the door. He went home hungry. Later he discovered it, cipki means pussies, more than one, and there he was, waving his money, two pussies, not the chips (American) or crisps (British). You have to send the right signals.

He moves to Elblag, Teutonic knights and turbine factories. At night, he slaps the bones on the table, with the DJ, who is also a mystic. The DJ shows him the hanged man, acceptance, an emotional release, surrendering to experience, ending the struggle, being vulnerable, giving up control, changing your mind, overturning old priorities, seeing from another angle, feeling outside of time, suspending the old order, a martyr, waiting for the opportunity, one step back for two steps forward, an about-face. Teutonic memorials, a buried sword, ancient romantic, and down below, naleśniki, easy to order, often satisfying, sweet or savoury, but mostly trying to fill up on the ham ones. The tower, around the corner, with little square windows, the turbine factory beside it, everyday working there, and then the Polish army, military English and tank manoeuvres. One day, in the pub next door to the naleśniki, a short Polish man pulled him aside, you can dance with me he said, and they danced, then when the song finished, at the bar with the beers, the small man leaned in closer, stick with me, he said, pointing to a strongman, the biggest man in the bar, the no neck type, stick with me, said the small man, I am

97

friends with the strongman. The strongman grabbed his full pint, downed it, belched loudly. The small man followed him home, and behind him the strongman, stick with me, said the small man. He had a flat above the bar, but he didn't want to show them, the strongman and the small man, walking in circles around the rebuilt old town, the strongman coming closer, the small man trotting along beside him, finally up close and personal, a swinging fist near his face, but it was only a fake, he didn't flinch, not rattled, he was trying to think on his feet, thank you, he said to the small man, walking fast, down a few odd streets, circling back, opening the door to his block of flats, quickly up the stairs, outfoxing them, no balcony for a smoke, waiting it out, no more local bars, just dominos and whiskey, a wise hermit.

He books the ticket to America, temporarily, to see his brother, an almost overdose, an almost lost arm, the heroin. His closest friend in childhood. He has to see him. Tired of traveling, tired of being tossed and turned by his libido, but also not knowing if he could go there. The painful memories, not belonging, no longer Mormon.

Late at night, he hugs his neighbours, the other English teachers. One, from Detroit, teaching for survival, starting over, a DJ in Poland, pudgy and manly. Another, from London, who doesn't want to have a mortgage or become a banker. The language school is proud to have him, the only black person in the whole town, tall and beautiful, meticulous. The Polish American, from Greenpoint, who left Poland when she was younger, for a new life in America, her doctor father left her mother, she grew up with her mother and her new partner, another woman, duplicitous. She is always saying masculine is not always bad, feminine is just as toxic. He hands off his small desk, with wheels, the centre of his existence.

The train clacks along, from one small station to another, with their little cafes, heavy overcoats, construction on the bridge, it takes longer than usual, and then the city buses, 15 kilos, his life belongings since leaving America four years previously, keeping it simple, a traveling hermit, the hanged man, he took it seriously, he didn't want to lose his brother, the sudden departures, so many, there are many splits in the weather.

His mother meets him at the SLC airport and they drive to her new home. His room, upstairs, very cosy, a rocking chair on the front porch, giant mountains behind them, snow on the ground, and his brother, downstairs, kicking the habit, exercising, his family not static but changing, his mother with the house and life she had always wanted, a simple existence, but also hard work as a cleaner, so many hours, her body aching, and the nest more comfortable than ever, the warmth in there, except for his father, something is breaking, sickly sweet, something forced, he gives him a fossil watch. Will you wear it, asks the father. He says he will wear it.

Stephanie, his ex-wife, with small son, her own house & new husband in the north part of the city, a graduate from nursing school, her original plan at 18, now achieved, 15 years later, and he is here, at her house, to collect some of his books, the last of his belongings, old friends from North Carolina. His brother Aaron approaching 30, fighting the addiction. Later in the week they visit the SLC library, a modern build- ing, an architectural wonder, with the snow coming down heavy, taking their own selfie, in the toilets, a sense of belong- ing, coming home.

On New Year's Eve, with his friend Andy also visiting, Devastator beers in the snow, the whole sky a blood red sunset. At Piper Down, an olde world pub, making plans for the future. Everything going better, his brother is going to kick it. They meet his brother's old friend, twitchy and need- ing a ride. They shared a cell. Avoided the mafia. Most of his brother's paycheck taken by the government, to pay his drug fines. Eventually his car repossessed, walking many miles with the groceries.

His brother Aaron, and also the rest of his family, the closest he has ever felt with them, an acceptance, he isn't like them, but also like them, everyone changing, he didn't expect it. They watch *The Hangover*, with his brothers and their friends, the beer ping pong, his first time, a baseball cap backwards, like an American. His brothers lift the couch he is napping on, take the pictures, feeling it, more American, now that he left it, just one more journey, to Turkey, teaching English at an American style university, he can save some money, return to America, plant his feet here, again, with his family.

The Mystical Country

Two kettles on the hob, one smaller and the other one bigger, how to make Turkish tea, and also the white cheese in the refrigerator, swimming in liquid, do you drain it. On his first day up the hill for the meeting, he is listening to compassion, a meditation. A wild pack of dogs run towards him. They circle around him, various sizes, very aggressive, the wolf hunting dogs. He tries to communicate a friendly energy. The smallest one leaps up, tears his jeans, from his buttocks to his ankles. Some teeth marks but no blood. How to react. They howl louder. A man on a motorcycle, a security card, races towards them and scatters them. He insists on a checkup, but there's no blood, you must have a checkup. Then the rabies shots, at the public hospitals. At night walking back to his flat & anticipating them, the return of the wild dogs, from the nearby forest, but instead the whining, late at night. The dogs being trapped and shot, safety and lawsuits, the wealthy families of students. He feels guilty. Maybe they only needed to threaten them.

His friends bring him the birthday cake, on one of the

islands, the candles like sparklers. They give him 18 candles, not 36. Someone reports him. He was not supposed to leave the campus, even though it was spring break, no classes or students. The head is a businessman. Please sign the letter, he says. A formal apology. Then later they find it, his review on the internet job board, even though it was anonymous. It was you, they say. He doesn't deny it. They print off another letter. His resignation. Please sign, they say. He moves into the city, near the military, teaches at a language school, enough for month to month living, no savings.

After the shower, a new ritual, body creams, he is drying out, faster and faster. The first cream, for the face, pink, French fancy, but not expensive, thin creamy, it sinks quickly. The second cream, thicker, super cheap, on his shoulders, neck, lower back (possibly the driest), his half hairy chest. Fresh oranges, squeezed in Ankara, over the bridge. Under the bridge, kokorec, chopped innards cooked on a griddle. Also the florists, various arrangements. At Starbucks he sips the latte, a warm tit. Across the road, a great buzzing, the children at the park, swinging and sliding. He lifts up his head, tries to keep his neck straight. The neck drives the body. Someone sighs next to him, breathy. Is this taken. He is sweating, he is not ready for it, too much preparation builds it, better to just jump into it, human interaction, trying to be natural is not natural. No go ahead, he says, pointing to the chair beside him, his heart overworking. The chair screeches, not lifted, a middle-aged man beside her, they share a slice of cake, chocolate and layered, the last piece gets gets smaller and smaller, they keep passing it back and forth. The man keeps scratching his stubble as he talks to her. He sits straighter, the blades of time dig into his back. Across the street at the florists, what to ask for. The florist makes an expensive arrangement. An embarrassment. He is a foreigner, supposed to have money. He asks the florist to thin it out. My vase is small, he says, in bad Turkish. It is still expensive, the florist cannot thin it any further.

When he leaves his job at the university they make a logical agreement, to move in & pay half the rent, if it didn't work at least she has some extra money, since her father owned the flat, a business deal, and if it worked maybe something more. The flat smelly, in the basement, in the old part of the city, but also authentic, near the military bases. The Turkish all-seeing eye. The drumming early in the morning, during Ramadan, before the sun, a call for breakfast, and the dolmus, crowded and dusty, handing your money through the people to the driver and then waiting for your change, not queuing up, the swarms, a different culture, also beautiful. In Istanbul, the call to prayer echoing through the old alleys, the layers of history, so many, a mystical country.

When they sleep together, she is worried. Is it too big,

she asks. It is flappy, another kind. No, he says, everyone is different. What is normal. In the deserts of Karaman, the sun reflecting off the shiny roof of the mosque, eating in the cafeteria, staying together in the city in a rented apartment, sex in the shower, the mobilya so many, couches and chairs and beds, and the dusty streets, an ancient place to wash your feet, and during the world cup no alcohol, a dry city, drinking coco cola through a straw, Turkish ice cream in the evenings. Everyone thinks he is from Germany, a blond foreigner, the only one with a Turkish girlfriend. It is, temporarily, a good feeling, the right mission, enjoying the country, not making huge plans for the future.

Don't break up with me, she says. Her only boyfriend for many years had left her, she felt ugly. I can't take it, she says, be gentle. He tries to be honest in the park, he will not stay in Turkey forever. They can keep each other company. She agrees to it, you don't rush it, love in the distance, it might come later, when you are not looking for it.

She takes him to meet her parents, her father a stern businessman and her mother plump and friendly, telling him to ash into her plants, it is good for the soil. Her sister married, living across from her parents, hiding her smoking, even though she is in her 30's, making fun of the covered women. A large picture of Atatürk on the wall, the father of modern Turkey, and also a reminder to keep Turkey secular, not embroiled in religious fundamentalism, a bridge between Europe and Asia. The Atatürk pens and ties and everywhere the posters, in every classroom at the university where he used to teach in Ankara, but not in Karaman. Karaman is something different.

It continues, for a few months, the same talk, many times over, in the park beside her house, after she dyes her hair bright blond, trying to please him with standard Barbie features, popular also in Turkey, even though he didn't hint or ask for it, she was trying to keep him. He tells her, for the last time, in the park near her house, with the children play-ing, he had realised she was waiting for things to change, they weren't only keeping each other company, she had introduced him to her family, the first time since her only boyfriend, and many years single, he was hurting her more by staying, they had different expectations, it was only the companionship, after months living together it wasn't getting any better, feeling less and less, no it wasn't her shy personality, no he couldn't assess it, give her things to work on.

He moves in with a couple, one from Poland and one from Turkey. They split the rent, cheap accommodation, near the main Mosque in Ankara, his own room. He climbs the many steps after teaching at the language school, the exercise very good, it is the real Turkey, not secluded on the hill at an American style university. The Turkish teachers feel worried, a whiff of something changing, Erdogan is giving the poor free refrigerators, but also, on the streets, another coup maybe coming, maybe U.S C.I.A. initiated, a take down and replacement with a U.S. puppet dictator, something dangerous. The Turkish teachers want European passports, to leave with their young families, they can feel it, something coming. He scans the ads for Italy & answers the ad for dog walker.

Bora

In Trieste, he imagines James Joyce, middle class or higher, like almost all artists and writers. He does not have the advantages, but also the advantages, coming from somewhere else. You can't help how you were born but what you do with it. You can only do so much but how much. He has twelve notebooks from various countries, but nothing congealing, someday maybe. He will not apply for American citizenship, or renew his alien card, he is not returning to America, keep living in Europe, free from student loan indenture, no credit cards or property, living simply, from one day to another.

Something called gnocchi with four kinds of cheeses, and also the wine with free appetisers, if you arrive at the right time. The hand drama, his first crush, the hand drama, something he doesn't have. He likes it when he feels it, his hands and mouth moving at the same time. The great journey, looking out to sea near the Piazza Unita, the Irish mermaid on his left arm, there are many ways to travel, and also monsters. Forever plowing the depths, and also moving. A nomadic existence, but also stability, forever juggling them, like everyone.

The water at night rippling black. What is below. Everything. The mind an iceberg but don't crash on it.

The Bora howls down the alleyways, blowing the laundry from the balconies. The two dogs, one a golden retriever and the other a pug, pull him in different directions. At the Scooby Doo cafe, his first Italian espresso. A real Italian pizza weighed by a master chef. Biting around the stone of the olive flesh, sniffing deep reds. He didn't grow up with it, the fancies. At Piazza Unità looking out to sea. Stay down there, underneath, where everything is happening, but don't forget to come up for air. He looks in the mirror, the shavings, do I trim it or grow wild, he thinks. Maybe he could become more Italian. What is an Italian. From the inside it is something else, or many things entirely. The bora howls some more.

He wakes up with her punching him, calling him a fucker, telling him she hated him. When he wakes her up to tell her, she doesn't believe it, he is only imagining it. Are you calling me a liar, she says? She takes a mattress and sleeps in the living room. No stay here, he says, it's your room, but she refuses. In the morning, feeling embarrassed, sleeping in her room while she slept in the living room, her ex-lover over with the groceries, her ex-fiancé sleeping in the other room. He keeps the razors hidden. She is a cutter & honest with her assessments, after every sexual act a score card, it is always good, but never a 10. Penis in the mouth, don't let it get big I like it small, she says. Her ex-fiancé cleans the flat. Her ex-fiancé's Italian mother pays the rent. An ex-lover cooks all the food. He washes the dishes and provides the pleasures.

Her supervisor calls her, when is she coming back to continue her research, a new model of the universe. Finally she is ready, he can go with her, up on the hill, with a great view of the craggy sea waters. On the way to the bus stop she tells him not to lean over, bad posture, walk straighter, walk straighter, she says. Like many countries the creeping insecurities, what was he really, how to act, where to put his eyes and his hands, how to walk properly.

In the evening another argument. He is not clearly defining his terms, what is collectivist and individualist. She shows him a Bob Dylan video from YouTube. Do you see, she says, the wind is blowing but his hair isn't moving. The perfect performance. She is looking for the product and he is looking for the process. He has discovered their differences. Another argument, very heated, no one dies from it. They mutually agree, it isn't working. He books the tickets for a return to Ankara.

His wild horses are running away from him, he decides to write the checklist. The pluses and minuses of London versus Ankara. He could move to London, reconnect with the poetry community, friends and community, how high do you rate them. He puts them at the top. The job situation roughly the same, maybe Ankara a little better since it was a university, maybe some better stimulation than a language school in London. Also the language, high on the list, even though it was a different kind of English, not the American he acquired, almost a foreign language, but closer to his mother tongue. What was it, Northern Irish, lowland Scottish mixed with Irish and English, also working class British, and with a larger percentage, maybe, the small town western American. Something is thawing. London is winning. He calls Pineapple, confirms it, yes he can stay with her. He cancels the plane ticket to Ankara. He is flying to London.

Love is to spoon as rock is to chip

There are so many books in her room, from Žižek to Taoism and Buddhism and Kerouac, cozy and warm, he starts to read them while she is attending her night class, especially the ones on mediation. He needs to get back there, the emptying and also the mindfulness, the letting go, and then in the evening, from around the corner, some fish and chips, loaded with salt & vinegar, the batter on the fish crispy, just like his childhood, a few beers, sitting in her room, the conversation real, sharing the pull out couch. Do you mind if I put my arm around you, and before long they are doing it. How easily it slides inside her, hand and glove. It is the only time he has ever felt it, the perfect fit, in mind and body, flourishing together.

How to keep it, or expand it, it builds, but also the worry, at the duck pond in Ally Pally, are you leaving or staying, they both have it, fickleness. They have to build it, the trust, her biggest fear is dishonesty. The search for authenticity. He finds the poetry community, the first time since North Carolina, new friends, a sense of belonging, also his writing, it is finally happening, the NY school poets, a new voice, more authentic, natural, from inside and also outside, explorations. They rent a cheap one bedroom, in Wood Green, North London. 700 pounds a month, from a Polish estate agent, one of the cheapest flats in the city, black mould and cold, but also good. Later, East London, a warmer flat, in the Docklands, Tower Hamlets, close to their friends for Friday night meet ups, but also rough, and, over time, exhausting, the survivals, what was basic and what was extra.

The fog rolls into the council estate and, in the distance, the red light blinks on top of the HSBC tower. Smudged grime clogs the windows from Commercial Road. He puts on some jazz music, a little like the wind, nothing too jumpy. For two weeks before the holiday he woke up early, his head full of plans, what ifs, how to make a decision, how to become more animal and a little less human. Just do it, like the slogan, and then pick up the pieces later. It is not what we have been trained for, regret is a sponge, it absorbs, how to wring it out. This door opens and another one closes, or, if you believe in the new theories, there are lots of doors, multiple floors and universes, so there is no wrong decision, just a decision. Weighing yourself down like a log but even logs float. Hope for everything but expect the worst, no that's not it, hope for everything but expect nothing, hope for someplace warm, another way to remake yourself, to call softly your own name. People exude love like the sun gives out heat. Love is a lot of applesauce, like water off a duck's back love runs off the human bacon. Love is to spoon as rock is to chip. He puts on the kettle, twists the knob, secures his robe.

The river doesn't have much oxygen, it is cheap as chips, preserving everything, Victorian, Elizabethan, even Roman, layers upon layers of brutal history, personal, and also historic, beside the river, on the east end, you can smell it, dippy egg and soldiers have always been a family favourite, it is cheap as chips, a soldier is a thin strip of bread, dip the soldiers one by one into the egg, the egg should have the top of its head removed, the bread should drip sunny.

They take the Megabus in the mega city and visit Amsterdam. Amsterdam has better oxygen, everyone cycles. The hostel in Amsterdam is really a ship, it is called The Gandalf, cheap as chips. The smoking deck is a good place for coffee, he wears a wooly. The owners provide a Polish breakfast, full of fresh veggies, polish pickles, bright red peppers. A pepper/ give it some wings/ a red firefly.

They live in the original Chinatown of London, before it was bombed by the Germans and moved to Soho, there are a few scattered remnants, but mostly monuments to finance, the centre of modern existence. In the jungle of the temples to finance, some art to cheer your existence, shiny pink petals, very large, maybe ten times their size, made of steel and glass, also shiny dinosaurs, with horns, the same size as the pink flowers, also made of steel and glass. Everything is steel and glass, he says. It was better before, she says. Better before what, he says. The dinosaurs surround the pink flowers, lifting their neck like a crane. All those lights without anyone inside, it makes me feel lonely, she says. A little like those scenes in a Hopper painting, he says. No not like that, she says, there is no woman with a hat, no all-night cafe, no sturdy wooden chair, teacup, no shaky hand about to lift the teacup, no human contemplating lost love, there is no love, it is devoid of the human touch. Yes, he says, devoid of the human touch, what is the human touch. Hmmmm, she says, these buildings were built by machines who were built by machines who were built by the human hand, they are two or more stages removed from the human hand. Yes, he says, we have to bring back the human touch.

They stand on their balcony, in the cheap seats, with a Lucky Strike, looking at the glowing towers of HSBC and Morgan Stanley, and sometimes, if the sun has made an appearance, which is rare, the solar panels light up above them, they have many plants lining their windows, they bring them to the bath to change their soil, feed them superfood, they want them to grow big and tall.

You grow a beard to protect your tie. Wear a tie to choke your neck. Eat thin pizza with cripple crow. Smell the flowers and listen to the blues. It is hard to beat a flute. What does a percussive flute sound like? 99% of people name the coconut as percussive fruit. The Duped Delight video claims JFK was a dummy, before he was shot, he was a dummy, strings around his thumbs. The official colour of London is grey. Colour therapy: red with green, yellow with purple, blue with orange. colour therapy: scorched and dusty green-gold, yellow-gold, & pink gold. Space therapy: using nine fingers on each hand, including the spaces. The alps: souped poles in a beer garden. The art of spacious living: a sigh from deep in the belly, sometimes a groan.

Pineapple returns from the shops in Wood Green. He is bent over, sobbing, the first time she has seen him crying. His sister, her voice so far away on the phone, and the thoughts, he should have been there. Feeling the shock and then the weight of it. Shortly after his own body giving out, first his knee, and then his back, and other body parts, the mortality.

He can't make the funeral but comes after. His brother Luke drives him to the grave site, a lump of grass, no headstone yet. Someone from the church donated the plot but they are waiting for the tombstone. He sits there, on the lump of grass, and wonders about the location of his brother. Is he down there? No he is gone. Somewhere else but where. He has all the philosophy and theories of death. His grandparents and friends had died, but this is something different, close to the bone. He had just acquired a new job, as an adjunct, at an American style university, mostly composition classes, but also a class in travel literature, hoping for something better, maybe a secure wage, but it didn't happen, a bit more than a shoestring, not enough to visit America, and now his brother gone, his best friend when they moved to America.

His sister organises the trip, from Utah to California, in honour of their brother. They drive through Hurricane, where his departure from the family had started, after his mission. The former Bishop's wife, across the street where they used to live, offers them a box of fresh peaches. She gives him the look after hugging him, disgust. He was supposed to be spiritual, lead the family, the same birthday as Jesus, a special mission, maybe someday a prophet or at least a general authority. It all fell apart when he returned home early from the mission. His brother with the skaters. His first taste of Angel Dust, and then more drugs. Could he have saved him? The room was locked, there was no getting out. They busted down the door and found his brother. Bloated. Reaching towards the door. It rocks everyone's existence. His other brothers show him the pictures, and also his mum, the funeral with bagpipes, an Irish flag, and eventually on his gravestone, Irish Aaron.

On the way to California they stop to ride a rollercoaster, near the border between Nevada and California, and he holds on tight, white knuckles, feeling his mortality more than ever, everyone wondering what they could have done different, sharing the guilt, spreading the weight around makes it easier. The peaches melt into the backseat before they reach California. The waves crash. His sister's husband takes the three brothers, one missing, to the most famous surfing spot, tries to show them, since he grew up in California, but the waves thrash them. Later, in the low waves with his brothers and sisters for a group photograph. His sisters are tanned. He is pale white, squinting into the sun, remembering Piper Down, the olde world pub, the last place he celebrated with his brother, when he was recovering from addiction, everything in front of him, with his new girlfriend, & later his stepson. The sliding back, one last time, the dose too large, and now gone. He is seeing America differently, an expansive country, especially the deserts, a kinship with them, but also the student loan indenture, after all the years impossible, he was only visiting, here now with his family, a reunion with tragedy.

His father brings him to the closet, take what you want, he says. There are a few pairs of jeans, some shirts, a stick of deodorant, his brother had pawned almost everything for survival, his old laptop, various clothes and compact disks and cassettes of punk music, especially Hot Water Music, the Utah government drug fines, survival, even the vehicle, pawned, or repossessed. He looks around the room, remembers the last time he saw him, Aaron slouched on the bed with a case of beer, watching the Dallas Cowboys. He said the Cowboys would win the Super Bowl, but it was a joke, then they did, later. The day before they had a farewell party, in the house, and his girlfriend, Tiyana, had made lots of homemade food, lettuce rolls with rice and meat, various treats, they invited some people over but their old friends were no longer friends, still on the heroin.

His father leans into the closet, smells Aaron's shirts, heaves silent sobs, take what you want, he says, I've already chosen mine. He takes the deodorant, RightGuard, a small sliver left from the roll up, also his brothers' jeans, baggy skater ones, far too big for him, and also his work shirt, Cool Valley, the family business, on and off, an air conditioning technician.

When he last saw him, at the door with the final farewell, his brother gave him the anti-anxiety pill for the flight back to London. Are you sure, he asked. You're my brother right. Also on the porch, late at night, at the farewell party, he should have said something more, it is too late, you can never plan it, not really.

His brother Luke has a tattoo with wings with Aaron's name. He has the Buddhist symbol of nothing. He remembers it, back in the kitchen, on the whiteboard, in felt tip pen, the list of their goals, a menu for healthy eating. Tiyana and Aaron were trying to put their lives back together.

He is back in London, never returning, but maybe again someday, a big reunion with his family, his mother knowing, herself an immigrant, far away from her family, and the lack of money to visit. He can live in Europe, simple and healthy, no children or debt. It is sometimes lonely. Immediately upon awakening he does the mental checklist, has he forgotten something, two hours later, depleted, planning, he opens the sliding glass closet. There are many hats: Ascot, Akubra, beanie, beret, and bearskin. Boaters, boonies, and boudoirs, fedora, fez, and flat cap, no balaclava. He looks out the window onto endless blocks of brown and yellow flats, it is the dead of winter, a coat, one from London, grey wool & itchy, but he prefers slippery, not too puffy, also neck huggers, variety, the perfect something.

Pineapple is still asleep, he brings the milky tea and toast, don't let the crumbs invade. They walk through their estate with the lingering smell of gunpowder and the springs of broken mattresses poking through lily white fabric. Along the way, the master scissors, more snipping, transplants for the living room. At Mile End park there is a mossy place, spermy beginnings, roaming clusters of people trying to get in touch with nature, or make secret deals away from the eyes of strangers. There is plenty of green moss, which one should we nab, a big one. Tadpoles stick to the side, hoping for the best. Back at the flat, they seal the ark, dry out the wet moss, scuttle through utensils to find the magnifying glass.

Black Friday came and went with a bombardment of

spam. They haven't done the Christmas tree and the foil. They haven't put up the lights, but the lights are shining on the canal. The canal is silky in winter lights. They heat up a potato. Flower it with corn and cream and chunks of tuna. All warm in the belly, she says. What did you do with my stockings, he asks. Look under the bed, she says. They look under the bed but there is noooo stocking. There is something else under the bed. But they can't see it. There are two red eyes looking back at them. She layers herself in colourful scarfs. Flag prayers to the wind. He pulls up his black hoodie. You have to protect your face from the wind. The cold wind can damage the skin's barrier. They cream their faces and hands and back and thighs. Ready, she says. Ready, he says.

They go for a walk along the Christmas canal. The sign before the tunnel says please honk before entering. They wait for a honk but there are no honks. It is a quiet night in London. When they pass through the tunnel, she unwraps the tin foil for the Christmas Cake. The traditional Christmas cake pulls out all the stops. The traditional Christmas cake is greased and stuffed with brandy. It is very heavy. They sit down in the tunnel.

There is something in the water. There is a large dent in the silky water. The large dent gets bigger and bigger. A spiked tail whips across the water. They keep eating Christmas cake while watching the lights on the Christmas canal. The

Christmas cake is heady. It makes the blood swim easily.

All warm in the belly, he says. They scrub you clean in the bathhouse, she says. All that dead skin. It just flakes away. The finest moment in the bathhouse is right before plunging into the water. Three white seagulls cross each other in the glowing white sky. Diving darting and circling. There is a yellow light inside the heart. Pull the string. Turn on the light. There are many creatures but today is mostly for the birds.

We are Pac-Men, gobbling up everything, hoping to eat enough pellets and find the special pellet (lover, song, movie, book, coffee table, trousers) to gobble up the hungry ghosts that are chasing us. There is no special pellet to save us. Death is far down, a sign, at street level, never on the upper floors, & they use a sheet to cover the deathface. The consolation is death and you never meeting, face to face, only in the abstract. This is compounded by the fear of something you can't imagine, or more importantly, usually, the fear of the pain that accompanies it. The death throttle, compounded, sometimes, by the fear of loneliness. Everyone you know will die.

The baby lizards run and stop, run and stop. The racer snakes can feel the heat and movement, but cannot see them. A game of tag with deadly consequences. The baby lizards must reach the rocks, & join the colony of adults, no one is coming to save them. The adults, a colony on the rocks, latched there, while the sea splashes over them, catching their breath, after a long dive to find algae and weeds, from the sea bottom, & also, if they are lucky, plants exposed by the low tide. From time to time, they eject, through their nostrils, a brine liquid, excreted by special salt glands, an adaptation to cope with the salted sea water. They are very good swimmers. Here come the racer snakes, & also the newly hatched baby lizards, stopping and starting, stopping and starting. Some of the baby lizards are eaten by racer snakes, & some of the baby lizards reach the adults, latch themselves to the rocks.

His brother's birthday two days ago with tributes and flowers on Facebook, he had to get off, couldn't write anything, couldn't say anything about his brother. Sometimes off to the side, with the petty fears and worries, and sometimes centre stage, what defines him, temporarily, and also often, shame daily, he didn't know what to do with it. A truck circles the neighbourhood with a loudspeaker, an announcement for the lottery, the weather frosty, the rats in hiding. He looks out the window, an old man and woman lean into the wind, centring themselves on the footpath. The man short and wobbly, his head bouncing, a little rubbery. They link arms. Empty wrappers and lotteries blow past their bunions and blisters. For many nights they warm each other's feet under armpits. Mashing the potatoes, chopping the veggies, sudsing the dishes. For many nights nature and travel documentaries.

There are many forces in nature. The future is in the wind.

They live in the biggest city of Europe, in a small flat, in the east, on a public housing estate, in one of the cheapest places in the city, borderline ghetto, borderline rich. Down the road is the financial capital. And up the road is also the financial capital. People come to visit and they pull out the blow up, there is no pump, so they, or both of them, have to huff and puff. They sleep on the floor. The living room is also the writing room and entertainment room. Entertainment consists of a computer screen and internet on a plywood desk, painted black, and chipping at the edges. It is almost the everything room, minus eating (the small kitchen) and sleeping (the ancient carpeted bedroom) and shitting (the mould-happy toilet room). Here is what you hear out the window: woo-woo. The woo-woo is very loud. It is not nee-nah. In France it is pin pon, in Italy it is nino nino, in Russia it is wiu wiu, and in the Philippines it is wang wang wang. The windows require frequent cleaning. They are very black from the busiest road in the biggest city in Europe. On the busiest road, in the biggest city in Europe, there are constant trucks, carrying supplies. It is called Commercial Road. They have fifteen plants, lined along the window, to catch the smog. Plants are part of the battle to keep your lungs pink. Try not to blow smoke on the gums. Blowing smoke on your gums is very bad. Your gums turn pale instead of pink. They turn a little grey. It is best to keep pink.

Here is one part of many morning routines: coconut wax swish between the teeth (15 minutes) salt water swish (25 seconds), electronic tooth brushing (3 minutes), cistus tea (anti-bacterial) (10 minutes), sage tea (anti-bacterial) (10 minutes), probiotic with millions of microbes (1 second), Nordic fish with vitamin D (1 second). On the estate there are many satellites to pick up channels from the home country. The home country is the near east, and sometimes the far east, Africa, and sometimes the continent of Europe. To acquire a taste for the new country there is Carnation Street. At the beginning of Carnation Street, a swallow is perched on the lightning conductor and the air ripples across the chimney. Carnation Street is very industrial. It is full of pink rollers and marshmallows. This is not the same in all European countries. Or, if the same, less the same.

They want to leave the financial capital, the small flat, the woo-woo, the happy mould and live in a non-financial capital, something cheaper. When they move to the non-financial capital, on the continent, and not on this island-slash-nation, people will visit them. They will get a bigger blow up, or a small second room, or maybe they can sleep on the balcony. There is much more blue in the new country. The fabric is more sheer. There is more summer there than here.

The windows open backwards, it is impossible to clean them, and often there is an invasion of insects, sometimes biting ladybugs, imported, non-native, and other times a lost bee, stunned, maybe by WIFI, other times plump flies, from above, hatched from the various nests of pigeons. Today it is the wasp, the same, or another one, climbing the window, when it gets to the top it falls down, begins climbing again, its little antennae moving left and right. Pineapple opens the window and fans it, it is a stubborn wasp, keeps climbing and falling, climbing and falling. She positions the book under the wasp & carefully elevates it over the ledge, it flies out the window, a lucky wasp. The next morning the same wasp, or another one, is climbing the window.

Tonight, at the Olde Cheshire Cheese, there are tiny rooms, musty & perfumed with Irish Canadian ladies. They began at the cockpit, another small room, and left that small room to enter another smaller room, and then another. They are now in the last small room, before the street, the holding room, with two boys, ginger haired, drinking cocktails. The Eggs in a Jar team drink till the very end. 11.30. Mike contracts and expands his hands, his hands are an air accordion and his mouth is moving, after three whiskies they don't know what he is saying. He is far from home, never at home, but also at home. Far from him the Tonka trucks, soda bread and egg yolks, red rock pilgrim trails and broad hats, crawdads in irrigation ditches, peaches mown into the grass, the gelled hair and choked tie of Sunday mornings, his name, his initials, his country, the future past and the present. Outside the streets are almost empty. They pause to look at St Paul's, a beacon of the city. In the evening it is hard to follow the names of streets, tucked away, high up, or nonexistent. Mike says he must travel an hour on the dark blue line back to his hotel, in the west, & all the vending machines are turned away, face the wall, ashamed, & the walls are flaking, the carpet is blood red, never hoovered, old prostitutes and workmen sit on stools with lagers, they don't clean the pipes. Alex has to go back to Elephant and Castle, but only for a while longer, he is engaged and has bought a house, in the deep south of London. They begin discussing the codes, there is no straight south, no S code, only SE or SW, & in many areas there is east, but no west, the streets around St Paul's are a labyrinth. How to get back in touch with your body. Sitting too long in one place pickles the joints. It is good to move freely from one place to the next and not lose all your energy. He leaves his foot on the ground, momentarily, before rocking forward to the balls of his feet, this gives more potential energy. His feet are snug and move quickly.

First of all, there's two. One, in Belfast, a big-hearted alcoholic, before his accident, a gardener. And also his father and his father's father father father. This is his biological. His wife died two days ago. She kept shit together, in the smoke-filled house, carpeted, overheated, John Wayne on the television, the Alamo. He met her twice. The first time ruddy and jolly, and the second, skin and bones. At the parades only a few sips of vodka. Weary in bed. And now, shortly after Christmas, gone. The funeral, in 3 days, on Wednesday. He has her father's hat, WWI, given to her father by his father. He still needs to wash it. He is supposed to call. He feels sticky. He's called and left messages, voice and text. He has to work up to it. He feels guilty.

His father, aged 20, and him, on a blue bouncy ball, with the handles. Dressed in hippy clothing. Happy. It doesn't matter if he remembers. He has the feeling. Love. He ran through it. The bull is coming. The bull is coming, they said. Watch the nets. Where are we. His biological left letters. His mum did not show him. She wanted him to grow up new, without the burdens. Years later, he got them. A small pile. A few letters. His father wanted to know him.

Diaspora aspirations forever shifting. Please circulate the air. What are you talking about? The brain. We've externalized it. It's very messy. To get inside the mind. Is that the story. There are so many minds and so little time. Is that the story. His inkwell runs dry, but not really.

His biological disappeared in 1980, 25 years later, a reunion, in Belfast. They spotted each other at the train station. Same shaved head, beard, glasses, eyes. Also, the same toes. Two of his father's removed, an infection. Two of his, then and now, hurting. It could be worse. The second reunion, the parades and bonfires and three-day drunken bender. Zombie on the stereo. It wrecked him. They walked around the Shankill and he puked into the gardens. No food. Liquid diet. Finally, at midnight, each day, a kebab. He couldn't stomach them. His father fed them to his plants, above the sink. It's good for them, he said. At 2AM, the nipple twists on the estate, a drinking club for Liverpool supporters. No one there. Do you like Johnny Cash. They couldn't get Johnny Cash on the jukebox. It ate the money. 12 lagers and mini bottles, white wine. Back down the Shankill, are you collecting money for the burnedout house, do you have a light. Holding up his father against the crumbling wall. The stares. Another Guinness. A few kebab bites. The leftovers for the plants. He slept squirmy, in the small room, with an itchy blanket.

He is not Jesus. He likes to tackle the person that tackled him. When he sees a father with a child on his shoulder, it hits deep. When he sees a father hugging their offspring, he buries it. Sitting still. Watching it. Non-judging. No one can find the original recipe. His fathers, absent, soften him. His fathers, absent, harden him. It went away. Is it coming back? Who knows. He is not a sappy story. He has a bad toe. He has a bad knee. He is tracing his ancestry. He comes from the ground. Pricked and scabbed over. Feeling empty, but not the right kind. Dulling the senses, but not the right kind. Moving slower more aware, but not the right kind. He's still here. One way or another. Trying to stay invisible. Reading over his head, trying to get clever to escape his fate. Does he have one? He stuck himself to it. The books. Finding yourself. No, losing yourself. The erasing. Also, survival. A way of being. Yes please.

There are many bends in the river. The Thames rolls its tongue against the crumbling gray bricks. The Thames holds its silt. The silt preserves the artefacts. To become silted is to: become blocked, become choked, become clogged, fill up (with silt), become filled, become damned. Unlatching the gate. Or climbing over. You might get away with a different coloured door. But mostly not. You shouldn't feel too special. Just lucky. You climbed to the top of the government waiting list. You could get different coloured milk tops from the milkman. That could make you feel special.

His stepfather grew up in Warrington, joined the British Army. A way out. Northern Ireland. He married his mother. In Bletchley, they went to the swimming pool. Hot chocolate, in the plastic cup, from the machine. I'll give you a pound if you go down the slide he said. In London, in the homeless hostel, a sip from his beer. Play Your Cards Right on the telly. Twisting his moustache and flexing his biceps, playing Mormon hypnotism, on Mondays, in Milton Keynes. In America, wilderness survival. Black powder rifles and shotguns. Then, snowed in. In the sleeping bag, hypothermia. Awkward bonding. He did not know how to hammer. When he worked construction, he could not find the stud. He is not a man. He is not a woman. Yet here they are. Father and son. The many failures and expectations. Unconditional. The confusions. His stepfather, on top of him, a few punches, his heart on his heart, beating too fast. He didn't want him to die.

Everything gets recycled. A banshee cries like a cat in heat. There is nothing you can do about the Banshee. The Banshee will come when it comes. There is no use waiting. It is better to admit the Banshee exists and then forget about it. You could send out all the not Banshee energy you want. The Banshee will still come. The Banshee can steal some of your life force. Sometimes for a long time. Sometimes a short time. Sometimes forever. If it is forever you are called the walking dead.

After the divorce and the death of his first born biological, his stepfather got a tummy tuck in Mexico and a motorcycle. Left the Mormons. Drove to South Dakota, in the middle of winter, with his ancient ancestors, to protest the Dakota pipeline. Now off the grid, stealing eggs from the farmer, in Utah, mostly high. Sleeping in his car, homeless, odd jobs here and there, he has joined a smaller group, left leaning. They want to change the world. It keeps changing. They can agree more now, than then.

Do you remember when you wanted what you currently

have. When time begins to pick up speed, the days grow shorter. He wakes up in the morning. Holds his breath. Late afternoon he remembers to breathe. To keep the game in motion. Trying to scrape off the layers to find something shiny or rusted underneath. Probably mostly rusty. But there might be some shiny bits too. Try to breathe, again, more easily. When you relax you can lean into it. Painted faces and spooky howling. Primal yelps. The mighty dust balls. It was only temporary. Bouncing back means moving forward. Long long ago, he owned a rubbish bin on wheels and wheeled it to the curb. He is not too big to fail. Paradise is very fickle.

Deep in the bowels of London, beneath a famous bridge, they are the second couple to arrive. The Groupon gives them one free cocktail, but not the fancy ones. Ah well, he says, gin and tonics, without the special floaters. The show is very fancy, they are not fancy, but, deep inside, there is an inner fancy. The show brings out the inner fancy, but not much. Top Gun wears aviator glasses plus washboard abs and shiny body skin, lap dances around wooden chairs, plus meaty bum wiggles and back clenching. Top Gun is Top Gun but the stage ninja is hidden, short and balding, he pulls off all the furniture from the stage, hides in dark corners. Then viola, he becomes fastest bum shaker. The sexiest dancer. There is no over the hill.

A mother's milk can beef up a baby's bacteria, important

gut bacteria travel from mother to child through breast milk to colonize the gut, over time a pound or two of bacteria live in your guts, they are ingesting millions of bacteria, from a capsule, they are the good bacteria, the bad bacteria live on sugar, at Paul's bakery they acquire a chocolate tart, rich and slippery, when they listen very closely they can hear them, the good bacteria fighting the bad bacteria, harmful bacteria can rapidly grow in your stomach, harmful bacteria can spell disaster for your bowels, they are trying to improve their mood with more good bacteria, the gut bacteria travel on the gut brain superhighway, but you do not want too many bacteria, or too little, or the wrong kind, get the right balance of gut bacteria for a good colony, it is important to develop a good colony.

Down the road a dog, black and white, a small nose, something shepherd like, it digs holes all over the communal garden. In one of the holes he finds a doll. Dolls have traditionally been used in magic and religious rituals throughout the world, the earliest dolls were made from materials such as clay, stone, wood, bone, ivory, leather, or wax. Is this a doll of bone, he thinks. It is not wax or wood or clay, where did you come from, he asks. The ancient doll has been found in the graves of ancient children. I believe in you, he says.

At Christmas, they cross the muddy platform with a small trickle below, a scraggly forest, then the square concrete houses with burning coal or wood, a full moon, a tyre hanging from a tree, swinging, no wind. Inside the mother is preparing another plate of cakes, makowiec, honey cakes, others, Magda deep throats her toothbrush to relieve herself of gas, there is a knock on the door, three flights down, come in come in, it is the annual Polish Christmas party, wine and beer for the women and mint vodka for the men, a record player with one crate, to the left, full of experimental sounds, some scratching and crawling, others popping and beeping. Let's have something to dance to, says Magda. Marta says no, she has found her space on the couch with a glass of sweet beer. Jozef finds the record, it's from 2000, danceable, Thomas Brinkmann, experimental minimal techno, the floor is wooden and slippery, a dip under the legs and out the other side, it is after 2 AM. There won't be another full Christmas moon for 30 years, says Pineapple. They walk back through the edge of the forest, but they didn't leave any crumbs. The trees bend further and further. Tyskie beer cans litter the ground, burnt out fires, makeshift camps, claps of thunder. Then along comes the boars, mamma boar and her three children. They hide in the bushes.

He sits on a park bench, in the Manhattan Estate, not far from Katowice centre, while Pineapple and her family visit babcia, a German prison camp survivor, living in Sosnowiec, kindly and warm. First come the moths, it is difficult to breathe without inhaling a giant moth, and then a woman sits next to him with a half dozen balloons. It is a windy day & the balloons keep pulling her off the park bench. She is half on and half off the park bench. He whispers all his secrets, all his fears. He tells her about his birthday party. I am sorry I missed your birthday party, she says. How old are you, she asks. He pulls out his small plastic wallet, shows her the expired alien card. Where did you get that face, she asks. His face was much bigger. It was too big for his body. It's expired, he says. It never expires, she says. He is not sure what this means but it frightens him. I am just trying to fit in, he says. Do you know vibrations, she asks. He tells her he knows vibrations. The woman takes out a piece of metal & a small speaker. She puts the piece of metal on top of the small speaker & sprinkles some sand on top. Then she dials some knobs in her oversized jacket. As the frequency gets higher, the sand begins to move into various shapes & patterns. This is your life, she says. He comes back from that world and touches his face. He is still here.

He walks past the war heroes and pigeons, fish and chips, Asian laundromats, swampy underworlds. He remembers the horse racing on the telly, with his biological, beers behind the bar at discount prices, the queen's head on the wall. No more queens, he thinks. He pees on water, in the bushes, outside the various factories of East London now turning into gentrifying art galleries. They chase the sun to the continent for cheap holidays.

The Polish holiday is in the mountains. They drink the sour milk (lumpy and sour and good for the belly) in a chipped cup, consume some squeaky cheese. They acquire a goral hat with seashells around the rim. The seashells show how far the people have traveled. They acquire a new pair of Polish slippers, handmade brown leather, tiny breathing holes, miracle cures.

To balance the stomach, grind starfish with coffee. Another miracle cure is the coconut. Melt the coconut between your fingers, drop it in your tea or coffee, rub around your face: nose, forehead, cheeks, chins, dimples, and eye sockets. When cold or stressed with low blood pressure, blood is redirected to the heart and away from the hands and feet. It warms the lower back, the middle back, neck, legs, and feet. The word coconut is derived from the 16th-century Portuguese and Spanish word coco, meaning "head" or "skull." It is a miracle to have coconuts. Lay down on the bed with your head against the feathered pillow. It is a miracle to have feathers. If there is a very small hole in the pillow you will awake with scratchings. The head is a tender jelly nut, an oily husk, a watery country, but, for now, mostly a fire country. The fire is now returning, a bulb that burns continuously, keep reframing the skull, bald, shaved, parted (on both sides), a fountain down the middle, cut with chunking scissors and spiked, a light bun, a little bun, a big bun, dyed, undyed, snaking down the back, behind the ears, over the ears, on the forehead, pulled back over the skull. It is a miracle to have a skull.

The young gather around the edges of the ancient wall in small groups, with cheap bottles of beer and pop music on their smartphones. Behind the walls are political slogans and a giant painted peacock, trees with glowing oranges. Behind the walls seafood cataplana, stewed and swimming in red. At a small ancient restaurant, an older lady raises her wine glass. She says nice to see you my friend. Four teenagers stagger around the square, one pushes a bike, the other boys repeat the sound. They walk to a warehouse & inside the warehouse heavy metal shakes the walls. Outside the walls there are fisherman hats and walking sticks, and down the road a favourite, a biblioteca that houses books & also wine. The wine is local from the north the south and also the middle. They drink the wine of the dark fruit, eat hare sausage, walk around the wall. On the inside, on the outside, the gate is always open. The wall is no longer a wall, it is only a frame.

Their hats came from an elderly lady in Loule. The elderly lady had a sewing machine in the corner and kicked out her feet to show the act of making, the act of spinning, it was the old ways, she didn't have any English, they didn't have any Portuguese, you can find your hat size, his is 63, the largest hat in the shop. Why is his head so big, he is humble but his head has something else in it. His shoe size is 46, but that's because of his toes, they are not the meat of the foot, toes are something extra, long toes do nothing for evolution, his big head does nothing for evolution, his head and toes are extra big for no reason. His left foot is bigger than his right foot, the right part of his face is rounder than the left part of his face, his left middle toe is more rigid than his right middle toe, the second hand of the clock is different than the first hand of the clock, the second hand is longer than the first hand, in short the hours are shorter than the minutes, his pleasant emotions are shorter than his unpleasant emotions. Buddhists say there are 121 states of consciousness, only 3 involve misery and suffering, why do we spend most of our time shuffling between those three.

Today, for a brief stretch, I was all there, he thinks, even though there were crowds, even though people were swarming (not walking), even though I was afraid of pride slash hubris before the fall, I walked big toe first, very straight, it didn't last very long. Yesterday he found the perfect shoe, made on the spot, in the old ways, the shoe is wide enough for the sharp slope from his big toe to his little toe, made from soft leather, a good space in there for his toes, also good space, here, in this notebook, without lines, and not there, in the other notebook, with lines, there is good space, here, with this Muji pen, and not there, with a generic hard to grip pen, there is good space, here, with the small leather briefcase and not there, with the usual heavy backpack, the backpack was purchased there, in the main square, the big one, not the little one, in Krakow, from a leather maker, in the old ways, birds were there in the square, it was summertime and sticky, cocktail time was there, in the Jewish area, over there, then, they were not cocktail people, then, and not now, the cocktail was exotic, like a peacock, & also, oddly, heavy in the belly, after 12 years with a blue backpack, full of student papers, it is nice to be here, with the bag in his hand, and not on his back, it is good to be here and not there.

In Faro the dogs walk themselves, they are very good navigators, strutting through the streets, guarding the doors, eating fish fingers, fish fingers are the hot dogs of fish, when they are ready to return home they lean on the yellow doors, the blue doors, the green doors, the door opens, they let themselves in, in Faro the pedestrians are cars, in the off season they cruise the streets very slowly, in the marina near the train tracks, a hot spot after school, during late winter, teenagers cruise with hot chocolate and cigarettes, late at night, middle aged women cruise for birthday parties, they sing the birthday song and drink punch wine, very jovial, a little bit South American, colourful, like maybe Brazilian, when cruising during the day they are sombre and European, but not miserable, everyone plays pocket music, no headphones, the pedestrians are crustaceans, hard on the outside, soft on the inside, in Faro there are blue tiles on the walls, geometric patterns, the sun sparkles, you can feel the sparkles, beauty is not static, it is the promise of happiness, Pineapple presses her feet into the sand, soggy, or packed with broken shells, for hours she tried to find the uncracked shells, the colourful shells, the big shells and the little shells, orange blue yellow and white, she slips off the wooly socks, carefully packs the socks with shells, & they arrive safely across the ocean, now on their windowpane, they look at the bright shells, the bright yellow curtains, try not to get wrapped up in the grey sky, grey buildings, smog & desperation, look at the shells, viola, the sea in their living room.

The grey squirrel, with very good smell, survives winter by hoarding nuts, they detect hoards through 1 foot of snow, sometimes they stay in the den for many days & venture out at midday to meet the flying squirrel who nests in groups during winter, they benefit from shared radiant heat keeping track of other squirrels through high-pitched cheeps, what do they eat, seeds hickory nuts acorns & wild cherry pits, the grey squirrel does not usually mix with the flying squirrel, this is mainly because they live in different countries, but the world is getting smaller, the thirteen-lined ground squirrel hibernates in winter, six months no food or water, they retreat to their underground burrow in October & reappear in March, they enter a state called torpor, use most of their body fat during winter, their blood loses all water to prevent ice crystals, the ice queen does not visit the thirteen-lined squirrel, & neither does she visit the grey squirrel or the flying squirrel, most squirrels live in hollowed out trees or underground, for a time they lived near the underground, the earth grumbles, & also rumbles, in the modern world in a modern city they get food from Iceland, Iceland are experts on frozen foods, they do not burrow their nuts underground, they wear many socks & many jumpers, on account of their cheap council flat, they are not a grey squirrel, not a thirteen-lined squirrel, they sometimes want to be a flying squirrel, but they are not squirrels, not squirrels.

Sometimes he has a body (rarely) and sometimes he has a spirit. He has a mind quite often. It goes and goes. He is trying to tie his mind, body and spirit together. The perfect package. It keeps unraveling. He thought once he tied his mind body and spirit together, he would be ready. There is no ready. Or there are different states of ready but no fully ready. One day he said OK. No more power hoovers. No more feather dusters. No more banana & jam sandwiches. No more wax machines. He travels in the middle of the night (to avoid the crowds), first a bus from the bus station with its dusty floors and roll over timetable boards and pretzel carts, then the ferry. On the smoking deck it is very windy. He has to pull up his hoodie. A man in pinstripes covers his face with a hanky. Some of the passengers have steel toes, others high heels. Some have made themselves into ancient Egyptians. He was putting the horse before the wagon. Now he is putting the wagon before the horse.

A sensual city with its fat sensual vowels, crumbling anarchic streets & canoodling couples. Scruffy cafes bursting with cream & wood fired ovens, taillights and clean sheets, flirtatious gazes and lovelorn graffiti. Te Amo Filomena. You are my destiny Fortuna. Marry me Stella. I dream of your kisses Balbina. Wait for me Ludo. Dead flowers & plastic jewellery. Skulls. Litters of bleached bones, faded photographs, lamb stew & bedevilled mirrors. Outstretched arms balance a sofa on a vespa. Outstretched arms haul banners of the Madonna.

The blues musicians pick their guitars, sing into the microphone. The make out couple tonguing and tonguing, one big wave. The pigs melt in the fire & little black butterflies go up the chute. They are the burnt ends, the crackling, the crunchy bits of days. At the end of a long set, the musicians slouch in the corner, cooling the tips of their fingers on their tongues.

At the monthly meeting of Eggs in a Jar, he is playing darts and eating peanuts, the bartender asks him if he has enough English salted peanuts. I have enough English salted peanuts, he says. You can never have enough English salted peanuts, says the bartender. How about salt and vinegar crisps, he asks. You can never have enough salt and vinegar crisps, says the bartender. Ditto cheese and onion, ditto Bovril beefcakes, ditto Marmite love spittles, ditto the jellied kippers skippers and eels, ditto sponge bread and sponge fruit and sponge chocolate and sponge clangers and bangers and mash, it is all space food, he says.

There are mostly middle aged, some older, some potbellied. Waves and penis nubs. Some with skin peeled back & others sheathed. Some curved & thin, others bulbous. Some firm chested & shaved, smooth bottoms. So many beautiful male bodies, some ripe, some tender. They are hidden ooglers, but they do not oogle too much. The two o's in oogle are two pairs of eyes. They try to keep their eyes from oogling. It is an all-natural beach, so they act all natural. They take the bus to city. When they drive past the slanted house of the famous artist, everyone tilts their heads. Upon exiting the bus, they head to the ATM. You stick in your card and you get your own private ATM. He sticks in his card and gets stuck. The people stream by as they bang on the glass. They are exhibit A. Finally, a policeman opens the door with a muffled snicker. The young boys and girls slip chiclets into their hands. You can only eat so many chiclets. No more chiclets. At the first shop the shopkeeper asks what they are looking for. How about a leather feather, says the shopkeeper. Yeah a leather feather, they say.

Is it all natural, they ask. It is all natural, they say.

They roam the withered veggies at Tesco. It is too expensive. The angry youth roam the estate, they have torn all the newly planted yellow flowers near the concrete football pitch. The next door neighbour gave them a money tree. They can hear her shout at her children through the walls to practice more piano, she wants, as a single Chinese immigrant mother, to give them something better. What is the discipline and how much do we need of it? There are so many bottle rockets and bodily ailments, but mostly the food and lack of sun. The body and mind not separate, you have to repeat it over and over, you deserve better. Or equally, you have everything you will ever need, like your body, how lucky.

We have forgotten our bodies in modern cultures. It is better to have a J spine than an S spine. A J spine is what you see in Greek statues and ancient cultures. In the west many of us are born with a J spine, but over time it becomes an S spine. This leads to many troubles, how to bend and sit. Here you see two Portuguese horsemen. One is slumped, head and shoulders forward, the other is pretty upright. What would most parents tell their children? Sit straight, upright and tense. You can only hold upright and tense for a few minutes and then it is back to slumping. We go back and forth between upright tense and slouching. What we really want is to be upright and relaxed. This takes a well-positioned pelvis. How is your pelvis? Is it well positioned? Your pelvis is your foundation. The best way to take care of your pelvis is to reimagine your tail. When you slump or slouch your tail sits under you. This is called tucking your tail. We learn to tuck our tails early. The way we cup a baby equals a tucked tail. The way we make our furniture equals a tucked tail. And thus we sit on our tails early. Our neural pathways are set. We are slouchers, & also tail tuckers, on chairs and on horses and in cars and even walking. Put your behind out behind. Do not tuck your tail. Get back your primal spine. A J spine. Not an S spine.

At the lunch table there is a man. He gets very excited about Vegas. You have to step into the casinos to cool off, he says. I played many one-armed bandits, he says. They give you free cocktails when you play the one-armed bandits, he says. Before you know it your eyes are cherries, lemons and sevens, he says. A thin man sits down at the lunch table. What's a one-armed bandit, he asks. A one-armed bandit is a slot machine (American), puggy (Scottish), the slots (American), poker machine or pokies (Australian and New Zealand) or simply slot (American). You mean a fruit machine, asks the thin man. Yes, a fruit machine. A casino gambling machine with three or more reels which spin. An expert uses multiple machines, he says. Interesting, says the thin man. Do you want to try a card game Friday night, asks the man. The thin man smiles. It doesn't hurt to practice, he says. He leans in a little more closely. Ever since the Chinese doctor he has been looking at tongues. The tongue is a map of the body. A history of the body. It is not what comes off the tongue but the tongue itself. The tongue itself doesn't lie. The thin man sticks out his tongue and rubs it behind his teeth. He is beginning to gleek. In general gleeking occurs when an accumulation of saliva in the submandibular gland is propelled out in a stream when the gland is compressed by the tongue. It is also an English card game for three persons played with a 44-card pack. Popular from the 16th through the 18th century. The jig was up. Another hustler. The tongue doesn't lie.

He finds 920 and knocks on the door, just a minute says somebody. The door opens. A little dog yelps. Back here, she says. He goes to the back room of the office. It smells like old mustard. Sit here and I will be with you, she says. He sits on the chair & they run through the checklist. All good, she says. Get undressed and lay face down, she says. He gets undressed and looks down. He is wearing his European trunks today. I should have worn my loosy goosies, he thinks. Do you have a rubbish bin, he asks. Over there, she says. There is a rubbish bin hidden under the chair. I like to keep it hidden, she says. He takes out his small wad and deposits it in the tiny rubbish bin, lays face down. Groupon is no good, she says. I never make any money from Groupon. She looks over toward the tip jar. He thinks about the change in the back pocket of his jeans, it is not enough for a tip, he thinks, is it better to give a small change tip or no tip at all, he thinks. His bones pop and creak, an old wooden boat swimming in oils. I don't know what I am going to do with this rug, she says. London is so expensive. What rug, he asks. Under the table, she says, there is gum all over the rug. She keeps rubbing and twisting his bones into shape. I am going to have to get special liquid, she says, special liquid is expensive. There is a deadly silence. My gum is in the rubbish bin, he thinks, it can't be my gum. Then whose gum, he thinks. I will need to cut the rug, she says. Or maybe I will have to buy a new one, she says. She does not say he put the gum on the rug and he does not say he did not put the gum on the rug. His bones keep popping and creaking, before long he is a spineless oily fish. He swims out the door, down Gloucester Road. Welcome back to your body.

She is drained from rain and cold bones and pushing papers. Maybe in Spain it is a little better, at least the weather. Also the directness, a different energy. Also cheaper to live as lower middle class earth dwellers. They visit Madrid, it is March and very sunny and they acquire small sunburns. She is in love with the sun, there is so little of it in London. Steppingstones, they say, while eating an American hamburger near the Avenue of the Americas. Back in London, at Tufnell Park, with their close friend Chris, they travel down the rabbit hole together. A saturation of images. Maniacal monkeys &

two-dollar radios. Galactic space adventures. The evolution of human consciousness. They all feel it. The edge of the bardo. He meets Stephen in the city. They walk over Waterloo bridge and walk around the Strand, munch on the best falafel in the city, nip down old historic alleys and side streets. The salvia keeps falling out of the roll up. They get the nips, one nip, two nips, three nips, another roll up, viola, they are in soho, it's historic. Massage, says a saleslady. No thanks, he says. Perhaps another day, says Stephen. They keep walking around the centre. Let's hop in here says Stephen. They hop in the French House with half pints and Ricard. Ricard is liquorice heaven, he says. Let's hop in here, says Stephen. They hop into a pub with sailor's ale. Sailor's ale is heaven, he says. Let's hop in here, says Stephen. They hop into wood warmed 600-year beer. Wood warmed is heaven, he says. Look, says Stephen, it's a mad hatter. I am always trying to find the perfect hat, he says. The mad hatter is named Laird. They crawl inside the mad hatter & flip through the pancakes. All the pancakes are tweed. It's historic, he says. It's classic, says Stephen. Made in England, says the mad hatter, but you are not tweed, says the mad hatter, your face does not say tweed. What does my face say, he asks. Let's find out, says the mad hatter. Here try another pancake, says the mad hatter. Here try another pancake, says the mad hatter. Here try another pancake, says the mad hatter. Here try another pancake, says the mad hatter. Here try another pancake, says the mad hatter. No more pancakes, he says, we are not pancakes. Here, says the mad hatter. Is it a fedora, he asks. It is not a fedora, says the mad hatter. Is it Frank Sinatra, he asks. It is not Frank Sinatra, says the mad hatter. He tries on the grey hat. What kind of hat is this, he asks. It is not a fedora, says the mad hatter, it is not a trilby, the structures of the two hats are similar but the trilby has a sharper crown and most importantly a much narrower brim. Yes, he says. Indeed, says Stephen. This distinction may seem minor, but we are discussing aesthetics here and a minor distinction makes all the difference in the world, trilbies use less material and are more forgiving of poor fabric, they are cheap to make and thus have become widely available. Yes, he says. A gentleman in a cheap trilby is saying I wanted a hat, so I just grabbed the first one I saw and considered that sufficient. Indeed, says Stephen. Right you are, he says. A man's hat brim should be in proportion to his shoulders, says the mad hatter. Sinatra was a skinny little guy with a narrow vertical-line aesthetic. Am I a narrow little man, he asks. You are neither a narrow little man nor not a narrow little man, says the mad hatter. A trilby on a big man looks like the reservoir tip on a condom. You are not a big man, says the mad hatter. You do not have to worry about the reservoir tip of a condom. He pops on the grey hat, pops off the grey hat. What kind of hat is this, he asks. It is your hat, says the mad hatter. It is your second skin. What kind of skin, he asks. It's a rabbit, says the mad hatter. Rabbits are good, says Stephen, you look good with rabbit. A rabbit is classic. It is habberdash, not balderdash. Dashing, says Stephen. Historic, he says. Classic, says Stephen. Made in England, says the mad hatter. It is good for your face, says the mad hatter, your face is longer. Everyone wants a longer face, says Stephen.

They order another biryani, leave Lahore with their bellies steaming with rice, sauces, veggies, spices, and delicacies. On a bench near Watney Market, popping the lids of the beer tins, leaning over to avoid the foam spills, Erkembode gives him a goodbye present, some stickers of a little monkey in a rain slicker to put on his new Chromebook. Also his outsider drawings. It all comes in a small brown envelope. Mail art. They walk towards Shadwell station, for the doom drone. Erkembode is friends with two of the band members, he grew up with them in Romford. Romford is where a lot of the British criminals were shipped off to Australia. So, the Australian accent is partially based on the Romford accent, in northeast London. At Layton, they follow the blinking blue dot. It is a ten-minute walk down the high street from Layton station. They walk for thirty minutes. It should be simple, 471 High Road, they just have to keep walking straight until they find 471 High Road. They keep walking straight for another hour. Do you know The Horse and the Buggy, they ask, over and over. No one knows The Horse and the Buggy. They keep walking. There is a giant shop, with red glowing letters. It says USSR. They have walked so much they are now in the USSR. All the lights are off. They can see food in the aisles, but they are written in a different alphabet, probably Russian. None of them speaks or reads Russian. They keep walking. They ask two men in a pub called THE HORSE AND THE HORSE if they know about THE HORSE AND THE BUGGY. It will take thirty minutes, if you walk fast, they say. They point straight ahead, so they keep walking straight. What was another thirty minutes? They had already been walking for two hours. Time. You swim in it, upstream and downstream. They move into a philosophical discussion about time that lasts two hours, but really two minutes. They keep walking. Erkembode doesn't want to miss his friend's DOOM DRONE concert. A little shack for a mini cab. THE HORSE AND BUGGY? Laytonstone he says, twenty-minute drive. They all look at each other. It was a fifteen-minute walk from Laytonstone not Layton. The mini cab across the highway and down many streets. They would never have walked their way to THE HORSE AND THE BUGGY, it is far too complicated, at least from Layton. At the HORSE AND BUGGY they put their hands on the bar counter. They can feel the wood shaking. Chris says it is a portal. Erkembode says it is a spaceship. There are twelve people in the whole spaceship and nine of them are in the bands. They have spiked hair with three different layers of colours. The three-layered hair people have part of their head shaved and dyed pink, another part long on one side and dyed blue, and another part spiked and dyed yellow. It is a very nice hair cake. They meet the father of the bass player. Erkembode knows the father. The father's son was Erkembode's childhood friend in Romford. The father is from Romford but originally Northern Ireland. He has been in England too long. He feels a kinship. They sing Irish rebel songs. They understand each other, far from home. Everyone huddles together. Chris asks the father if anyone's organs had exploded at a DOOM DRONE concert. The father says not that he knows. They wait for the portal to open.

He is sitting in the basement of a building at Richmond American University with a tiny heater, cold toes and no windows, waiting for his students at the writing centre, when he gets the phone call. He is going to become a father. It is not the reaction he is expecting. He is excited and hopeful. A new life is beginning. But he feels the fear of lack of finances, thinks about a better job, some kind of security. They don't have any family in the city. Their families are in Poland & Utah. Do they give out free nappies? Somehow people have babies. He imagines pushing the pram, changing the nappies. He sees fathers with babies on shoulders and imagines the baby. He sees fathers holding the hands of their toddlers and imagines the future. Bedtime stories and the exploration of nature. The open wonders. He wants to do it better, but what about the money. What was a good living for a baby? They pay the money for a private doctor. Pineapple lays down on the table, cold gel on her tummy. They scan for the baby. Is there something on the black and white monitor? Dots and lines, something blurry. They count back the days to Christmas in Poland, the date of conception. It is not showing. When will it show? They visit the doctor three weeks later. There is something on the monitor. You have to squint to see it. They hold hands and imagine the future. Sorry, she says. The little bean isn't sticking. They feel empty. Something will be released from Pineapple's body. Something gone, never there, almost there, a different life. They are leaving the country.

Dream Dust

It is mostly musty. They are constantly fighting various invasions of cockroaches. Spanish paperwork to accomplish small tasks. Even the changing of dollars to euros at a kiosk requires three stamps, various forms, a passport and a fingerprint. Their health is better than London on account of fresh veggies and sunshine. The great pleasures and frustrations and sickness. Pineapple visits the emergency room with stress and body breakdowns. There are lunch specials and nice wine, free tapas. They find the best places. The sun sizzles them. Trips to the seaside in Valencia and Alicante in the off season, the great sea spray, feeling the juice of it. Then the flat floods from a broken boiler. Then the refrigerator breaks and the landlord orders a new one. The new one doesn't fit. They have to keep the broken refrigerator in their small living room. It takes most of the space. For the first time in their lives they are outside more than inside. A slow return to the body. It is easier to be lower middle class than London. They fly to Poland for Christmas.

Seat belts buckled and unbuckled, seats claimed and

unclaimed, the carry on, is it too heavy, is it over the limit, they have passed inspections, can it be lifted over the head into the compartment, should the coat go under the seat or above them, everywhere is dirty, there is so much buzzing. He is wearing his wooly, sweating, so stuffy, please circulate the air. It is Christmas Eve Eve, the tail end of the year less than pleasant, but also, in spurts, pleasant. The airplane has started its engines, preflight announcements in English and Polish, a 3-hour flight. Pineapple's dad will pick them up in Wroclaw, and then 2 hours to Katowice. From Madrid it was a few changes, no buses, not like before when they lived in London. Of course, near or far, flying is an all-day venture. Should he strip down his language or inflate it?

He awakes from many stories, whose stories, I remember them, so I think they are my stories, he thinks. Cling wrap keeps the foodstuffs but not forever. Everything gets recycled, metaphor: a moving company. Outside the window, here in Poland, more specifically Katowice, more specifically the Manhattan Estate, near Piotrowice, the sky is monochrome, and the birds, two sets, are circling, in formation. Down below (the 7th floor of 15), a small playground, no one is playing. It is Christmas Eve, everyone is waiting for the first star, no snow. Igor's presents, bright red wrappers, are slouching on the couch. Plan ahead, everything closes at 2, maybe 2 packs, or 3, Lucky Strikes, niebieskie. The Christmas dinner, on the eve, and not the day, with three kinds of soups and 3 kinds of fishes, many cakes, pierogies. I think they are my stories, he thinks, they are nobody's stories, so many stories. Here is a story. When I awoke this morning, a plate of sausages was waiting for me, also, various dream states and erections, it was very pleasant. The sofa bed, hard, simple, orderly and good. How to show gratefulness in another language, with limited vocabulary, bad pronunciation. Here is a story, does it need a bigger conflict, why only one when there are so many, why not spread them, little crests and valleys, it's in my body, a western symphony, or something smaller.

He sneezes into the new climate, there are new airbornes, various germs, another conflict, but here, also sanity and order, to think clearer, white lights on the small festive tree, white lights inside the crystal, 365 white lights inside the white snowman, plus red, gold, and green balls, plus silver tinsel, plus a miniature Santa in pointed hat with small white lights, it is colour light therapy, this is the magic, he thinks, simple is beautiful, grotesque is big, America is big and bardzo grotesque, here, in this country, it is grey, but I am dry, it is not London, also, the people are loyal, to get inside the mind, is that the story, there are so many minds and so little time, is that the story, my inkwell runs dry, but not really, is that the story, all-natural: you have to search for it, plastic, while convenient, ruins everything, wooden blocks more natural, but not too many on the account of the trees, you can't win, is that the story, go green, especially for Christmas, Igor has wooden presents, but also, in moderation, plastic, getting and spending, the centre, where is it, is that story?

Where to, says the bus lady. He wets his whistle. The centre, he says, in OK Polish, the good, the bad, the ugly out the window, a lady sits next to him, tall, maybe lanky, dangling all naturals, very serious, I am seeing my cousin, she says, so far, the city wall is crumbling, it is a tourist centre for selfies, my cousin, the knitter, says the lady, pulling out a well-woven hat, very expert, so many kriss-kross patterns, very good spinach, says the lady, speaking vegetarian and giving tips for places to eat, he abstains from fidgeting, yanking his nose hairs, passing gas, do I like vegetarian, he thinks, a beard, no belly, shaved on the sides, minimal hipster, the new generation, mostly vegetarian, his head, it opens, the tools, wrench, pliers, cutters, but, most importantly, the ruler, not what, but how much, a nip here and there or something long and slippery, that's my stop, says the lady, he measures the distance, not far from the centre, sometimes you go somewhere, other times nowhere, sometimes somewhere is nowhere, and vice versa, be careful of tying your head into knots, he gives up his seat, it is only a short distance longer, he wedges himself between them, one man reeks of corn puffs, another musty beer, suddenly a buzz in his pocket, did you make it, she asks,

I almost made it he types, I am still trying to make it, I may never make it, when will I make it, the chime, the buzz, the swipes, the brain, we've externalised it, it's very messy.

He showers to shake out the dream dust, last night, Bob Dylan died right before the concert, everyone was waiting, the last of the legends. What is the story, the sky is gunmetal grey, blank slate grey, there are too many words on the planet, clever, charming, and full of life, not today, not ever, maybe somewhere the charms are waiting, save the charms for later. Cheap simple living, 43 on a student salary, still making a way in the world, still breathing, not homeless or starving, a simple funeral in the future, will the Spanish or British or Irish pay for it, I am not working my guts out for it, everyone, probably, in some degree, with the thoughts, why work so hard for a casket.

On the wall, a man and woman lean to the right, in summer hats, painted by a distant relative, a hopeful adventure, long dead. Today is babcia day, 86 with aches, who wouldn't, concentration camp survivor, long time widow, in summer, the grill, family gatherings with blood sausages and kielbasa, in winter, makowiec and wiśniówka, she still lights the old stove, on the table matrioszka, from largest to smallest, over 100 in the wooden cabinet, the newest, niebeska, with white flakes and large mother shawled face.

Forever shifting, diaspora aspirations, the Polish, the

Irish, no, not the English so much, the many planets, maybe universes, wrap your head around it, we come from the Milky Way. At the opera house, very dark, an orchestra of saw music. At the wooden pub, eskimos in the toilets. Not eskimos, he says, Greenlanders. They nurse a beer outside the pub. Two older ladies tap Pineapple on her forehead, wave their hands around her halo. On the wooden porch, some broken glass, be careful, says a face, well-worn with the tree rings of history, the children are coming tomorrow. They walk through the village. Through the trees, and onto a busy street, back to civilisation, regular feeding times return sanity, but only temporarily.

When slowing down, he dreams more intensely. Who the fuck are you, he asks. The man in his underwear keeps climbing. A strong storm, a variation on the familiar. All the leaves crispy, rattling down the hallways. He gets the shivers, from crown (left side) to toes, at least, currently, no eye twitch, for so long the eye twitch, & his stools slowly regaining the bile. The right foot, under the ankle, near the arch, still burning, the knee pops, normalised, only there when you pay attention to it. Last summer the lower back gave out, the muscle relaxants and pain pills, no more anti-depressants & anxiety medicines. He sips the green tea, tries to breathe again more easily, when you relax you can lean into it. The man in his underwear keeps climbing.

His mind fastened/unfastened elsewhere. Pleasure maintenance. Become insane for sanity. In a sick culture you have to find another way of measuring. Upon closer inspection, the winners born winners, the parents professionals, university graduates, rarely the food stamps. Everyone always something better, more accomplishments. Entitlements, male and female. Art, who has time for it. Working class murky origins. Most days he forgets, but on holidays he remembers. There are so many ways to feel it.

Marta and Pineapple have to pee. They find their spot to squat, no onlookers, quick and not so easy. They are outdoor experts from long nights at the local sailor's pub. The owners, old timers, real sailors, traveled the world with many stories. Marta and Pineapple visited often. Now, a wall of bottle caps behind them. The pub, well branded, a dark hole, table football. He is offence and then defence and then offence again. He is better at defence. Pineapple scores all the goals. After much drama, the rising action, the tie at the peak of the action, and then, the gradual decline and resolution, they become winners, another round of cheap beers, more shots of wodka.

Do you remember when you wanted what you currently have. He imagines his bookshelves. When I hunted that one (pointing to the shelf of contemporary fabulists), I was looking to bring back the magic, when I hunted that one (pointing to two shelves of NY School poets), I was looking to make my mouth more American and free, when I hunted those (point-ing to the shelf of Lydia Davis), I was looking for clean breezy sentences of hyperreal absurd existence. When I hunted that one, (pointing to the shelf with all of Lukas Tomin), I was looking for permissions and validations for the absurdity of existence.

He unzips the smart phone from his pocket, a ding, some-thing to remember, from five years ago. Do I like it, if I liked it then, do I also like it now? He searches Amazon, if I like this I must like this, if I like this I must like this. The sum of my purchases. The computers are always guessing. Wrong, he says, delighted. I don't like it, you can never get me. Today, post Boxing Day, on a wooden chair with a blue blanket for back support. A Polish comedy on the giant telly. Pineapple and her mother and father very happy, the most generous and loyal and kind people really. He doesn't have the language, hopes they can read it, somewhere, on his body. He sits back, in the corner, next to the blinking snowman, where, six years ago, he composed a story, his first fable. The frizzy hair on his head. Today, per always, he is ruled by static electricity.

At the indoor playground, with 20 kinds of chocolate, Trele morele, the muds of my childhood and raintears, he says, smudging the windows. In the playground, a catchy Polish bear song, it is hard not to sing along. Now a song about a magic kingdom and a dark pink room with a magic castle. Little bear, real name Mikolaj, age 5, is collecting Go Ninja! Legos, but due to high demand, has settled, temporarily, on Star Wars. He wears very fine glasses with pastel rims. Mikolaj, the lego collector, is running through cookie monster obstacles, also, down the blue and pink banana slides. The adults are waiting for Amaretto coffee.

They are happy, with the weather and cheaper living of Madrid. Meggie Szu and Jozef, expert climbers, very good at fitting their fingers and toes into cheese holes, are happy with their new baby in a mystical forest. Marta is happy, in transition, a new flat on her own, still in the relationship with her Italian vegan. He drinks his amaretto coffee and sits on a turquoise plush chair. The coffee is not very coffee, it is weak and extensively sweet. How many sluggish keep drinking, peak at New Year's Eve and crash on the day. The tradition for New Year's, in London, was the Prospect of Whitby, low key, the old noose out the back, with John and Gosia. They will spend New Year's, for the first time, in Poland, with friends in the enchanted forest. They will listen, per usual, to exper- imental records and drink enchanted wodka with enchanted finger foods. Space is the place, everyone needs it.

Do I know the zeitgeist, he thinks, I don't know, but I feel it, or I don't. What is iconic? Tootsie rolls, an older zeitgeist, coca cola, for some people, in many places. He does not drink coca cola. 1985 in Milton Keynes, the tootsie rolls, handed out by Mormon missionaries, iconic and also histrionic. They led, mainly, to American immigration and Mormon conversion. No, not led, correlation is not causation, the academic mantra. Between worlds, robotic dancing, spinning on cardboard, and trying to move his mouth like an American. Sharp and sour sherbet pouches with a white dipping stick, pop rocks popping on the tongue.

Snow has fallen, finally, and now melting, already. Pineapple has built a snowman with Igor and now, in the kitchen, with her parents, rolling out the pierogi ruskie, the father, aproned, with python arms, the mother soft smiling and sprinkling, the daughter, Pineapple, rolling out the dough. He takes a picture. Keep it a secret, says the daughter, once someone knows, they disappear very quickly, everyone is in love with pierogi. He saves the pictures for later.

He continues with many episodes, a Doctor Who marathon, with very good moral lessons. How can I make my eyes more alive, he thinks. He doesn't remember any lessons, as a child, with Doctor Who, in the 70s and 80s. He only remembers the Daleks. The fear of the Daleks. Seek and destroy. The unconscious and the environment and the political all wrapped into a show. The last cosmic whale carries the happy freckle clusters. The king is torturing it. How very appropriate. The beast below is humanity's friend, how to nurture it. The starship travels faster.

Downtown Katowice, Muzeum Śląskie, a parade, a liber-ation, a freedom, an explosion of play and colours, the neo-avant garde of upper Silesia, psychedelic, from the 60s and 70s, animus and anima, Jungian explorers. One of them, Urszula Broll, still living, painting and exploring in the moun-tains, a wise hermit.

The mother and father are recording bird sounds into the phone. Barszcz, fresh, with dumplings, for New Year's Eve. The hair falls down, across the eyeballs, but at least there is plenty of it. Lately, he gets the beer spins easily. Today in Hipnoza spinning wheels & jazz. For the hungry, a river of cheeses, to grease down the belly. Later, the fireworks, many colours, a magic garden. To build better colonies, they crowd around.

The latest news, N. Korea, per usual, nuclear weapons, and South Korea with an olive branch for winter Olympics, a Bronx fire, record freezing in the eastern U.S., hard borders or soft borders or no borders for Northern Ireland and Brexit. Stiff neck and eyes, a new LP, from Jozef and Magda, Ariel Pink: Haunted Graffiti. Currently, the sky, clean slate grey. Szczęśliwego Nowego Roku. Igor at 1 1/2 years old, likes being carried and grunts softly. Unwrapping the Christmas choco-lates and placing them into the mouths of adults, yumyumyum he says, for encouragement. The joys of discovery. The phone in his pocket vibrating, he does not want to answer it, forever.

It is 2018, what happened. Where are we?

Pineapple lifts Igor's legs up and down, one leg, then another leg, then two legs together. Pineapple is exercising Igor. Magda is mushing his food. What is the meaning of Igor? He is a Scandinavian folk god. He is fire. He has come to free the people from slavery. Igor sneezes. It is a tiny sneeze. His burping bib has yellow owls. Today is Igor day. He stretches his arms above his head, it is the sign of victory. He curls his fists against his cheeks, it is the sign of thinking. The world of Igor is a mystery. It is 6 degrees.

ACKNOWLEDGEMENTS

A warm thanks to the editors of the following journals for publishing excerpts from *Never Mind the Beasts* (sometimes in different forms):

Tin House, Fence, Sprung Formal, Cosmonauts Avenue, Ohio Edit, Public Pool, Lighthouse, Gramma Press, Versopolis, Nice Cage, Dream Pop Journal, Plaster Cocktail, Alice Zine.

Some of these stories appeared as a chapbook entitled *Mu (Dream) So (Window)* from *Poor Claudia*. Much thanks to the editors.

Special thanks to Ewa Rasała, as always, for the love, companionship, and visionary insights.

Also by Marcus Slease

ANTHOLOGIES

Best British Poetry 2015
Dear World and Everyone In It

POETRY

The Green Monk
The Spirit of the Bathtub
Play Yr Kardz Right
Rides
Spanish Fork
Mu (Dream) So (window)
Smashing Time
Hello Tiny Bird Brain
Balloons
Primitive Pianos
Godzenie

Printed in Great Britain
by Amazon

41693161R00106